I have always been delighted at the prospect
of a new day, a fresh try, one more start,
with perhaps a bit of magic waiting
somewhere behind the morning.

J. B. Priestley

About the Author

Ellen Dugan, also known as the Garden Witch, is a psychic-clairvoyant who lives in Missouri with her husband and three teenage children. A practicing witch for over eighteen years, Ellen also has many years of nursery and garden center experience, including landscape and garden design. She received her Master Gardener status through the University of Missouri and her local county extension office. Look for other articles by Ellen in Llewellyn's annual *Magical Almanac, Wicca Almanac,* and *Herbal Almanac.* Visit her website at:

www.geocities.com/edugan_gardenwitch.

7 days of Magic

Magic

Spells, Charms &
Correspondences
for the
Bewitching Week

Ellen Dugan

Llewellyn Publications
St. Paul, Minnesota U.S.A.

FIRST EDITION
First Printing, 2004

Book design and editing by Rebecca Zins
Cover design by Gavin Dayton Duffy
Cover images © Photodisc, Digital Stock, Brand X, and Digital Vision
Tarot cards from *The Medieval Enchantment Tarot* © Nigel Jackson

LIBRARY OF CONGRESS CATALOGING–IN–PUBLICATION DATA
Dugan, Ellen, 1963–
    Seven days of magic : spells, charms & correspondences for the bewitching week / Ellen Dugan.—1st ed.
        p.   cm.
    Includes bibliographical references and index.
    ISBN 0-7387-0589-6
    1. Witchcraft.   2. Magic.   I. Title.
BF1566.D84 2004
133.4'3—dc22
                                                                            2004048422

Llewellyn Worldwide does not participate in, endorse, or have any authority or responsibility concerning private business transactions between our authors and the public.

    All mail addressed to the author is forwarded but the publisher cannot, unless specifically instructed by the author, give out an address or phone number.

    Any Internet references contained in this work are current at publication time, but the publisher cannot guarantee that a specific location will continue to be maintained. Please refer to the publisher's website for links to authors' websites and other sources.

    Disclaimer: The purpose of this book is to provide educational and historical information for the general public concerning herbal remedies that have been used for many centuries. In offering information, the author and publisher assume no responsibility for self-diagnosis based on these studies or traditional uses of herbs in the past. Although you have a constitutional right to diagnose and prescribe herbal therapies for yourself, it is advised that you consult a health-care practitioner to make the most informed decisions.

Llewellyn Publications
A Division of Llewellyn Worldwide, Ltd.
P.O. Box 64383, Dept. 0-7387-0589-6
St. Paul, MN 55164-0383, U.S.A.
www.llewellyn.com

PRINTED IN THE UNITED STATES OF AMERICA

Other Books by Ellen Dugan

Garden Witchery: Magick from the Ground Up
(Llewellyn, 2003)

Elements of Witchcraft: Natural Magick for Teens
(Llewellyn, 2003)

Forthcoming

Cottage Witchery: Natural Magick for Hearth and Home
(Llewellyn, 2005)

My mother always told me I'd be a late bloomer . . .
This book is dedicated to all of the other "late bloomers" out there.
Believe in yourself, follow your dreams and remember this:

It is never to late to be
what you might have been.
George Eliot

Contents

Monday 27

Tuesday 53

Contents

Thursday 105

Friday 133

Contents

Acknowledgments

For the lovely ladies at Llewellyn—New Submissions Editors Megan Atwood and Natalie Harter, for the fun we had brainstorming on the idea for a "little book of correspondences." And a special thank-you goes to my editor, Becky Zins, who enthusiastically rubs her hands together and dives right into my manuscripts.

For my family, who surprised me with the depth of their support and pride. To my sister, Julia, and brother, Scot, and their families. A special thanks to my Aunt Marti, who showed up to so many of my book signings and then decided to study and see for herself what the Craft was really all about.

To my folks, with love. Thanks, Mom, for taking me out for lunch so I could clear my head and laugh and talk. I couldn't have gotten chapter four finished without you! Thanks, Dad, for giving me good, practical advice. And I'll keep working on filling up that bookshelf of yours. Your support always brightens my day.

To my husband and three teenage kids, my own personal cheering section. Thanks for the loving support, the encouragement, and for looking over my drafts. You guys didn't even sigh when I started another book. You just braced yourselves, booted me into my office, and closed the door behind me . . .

My god, you are all so brave.

Write it on your heart that every day
is the best day in the year.
Ralph Waldo Emerson

∂

Introduction

The Bewitching Days of the Week

Magic is all around us at all times. Enchantment can be found in each moment of every day of our lives. In this frantic and crazy world that we live in, it is more important now than ever to stop and take a few moments for yourself and your magic. Set aside some private time just for you, each day. Then use this personal time to connect to the wonder, divinity, and magical energies of that specific day. If you've got only ten minutes to spare for magic, then use every bit of that time wisely.

Magic doesn't always have to be complicated. You are not any less of a witch if you choose to keep things straightforward and basic. Who says you have to spend an hour to set up and then perform your spells? If you keep things simple and practical you'll enjoy it more. And, basically, you'll be working magic more often. Magic isn't limited only to the Sabbats and to the occasional full moon; magic happens twenty-four hours a day, seven days a week.

Every day is a bewitching day, Sunday through Saturday. Each day holds its own planetary correspondences, deity associations, magical energies, and applications. A clue of how these magical traditions started is to consider how the days of the week got their names in the first place. Sunday is obviously named after our closest star, the sun. Monday was named after the moon. All of the other names for the days of the week are actually inspired by a combination of the old Roman and Norse deities and mythologies.

Each day of the week has its own energies and specialties, and the day itself may affect people in different ways. For example, do Mondays make you cringe? Why? They are not always the start of the work week. For those of us who work weekends, Monday is just another day. It is, however, the moon's special day of the week. What kind of magical work could you possibly perform on a Monday? Well, on that sacred day of the moon you could work for increased psychic abilities, or you could connect with a lunar god or goddess. What do you suppose would occur if a full moon happened to fall on a Monday? Hmm . . . this could bring about extra magical power and bring a lot more *oomph* to any lunar spell. Sounds like a double whammy to me. What about you? How could you use this information in your magic?

Techniques for Newer Witches

Over the years I have met many newer witches who are often confused and overwhelmed by daily magical correspondences. They rub their foreheads and

give me a pained expression as they ask, "Tuesdays are for what?" Goddess knows I've fielded this question many times with my circlemates and their kids. Some magical practitioners take one look at those massive correspondence charts and planetary hours and break a sweat. I can totally sympathize.

While serious astrological information makes my eyes cross (I think it reminds me too much of math), you can still easily learn more about the individual magical associations of all the days of the week. This information can help you figure out how, why, and when magic works the way that it does.

Inspiration for Experienced Witches

For those witches who wonder what the point is of relearning what they perceive to be very basic material, try looking at daily correspondences in a whole new way. It really doesn't matter what is the age of the experienced practitioner, whether you are in your late teens or in your seventies. Many experienced witches have trouble working successfully with the daily magical correspondences, so they face boredom and burnout. Whatever scenario you are dealing with, either is frustrating.

The topics covered in this book—the daily correspondences, tarot card associations, and other natural accessories—are like building blocks. You can successfully add this magical information to the Witchcraft that you already practice. Before you know it, you've increased your knowledge of the Craft, expanded your understanding of magical correspondences, tried your hand at creating some of your own spells, and stepped up in the ranks.

How to Use This Little Book

This book is set up into seven separate chapters, one for each day of the week. Within these chapters you will find a listing of the specific magical correspondences for the individual day. Each chapter is also broken down into seven enchanting sections. These sections are:

At-a-Glance Correspondences: A quick reference list for you to check out. An at-a-glance listing of the bewitching accessories and natural items that correspond with that particular day of the week.

Daily Magical Applications: The specific captivating attributes for the featured magical day. A smidgen of history and lore about the highlighted day and how it got its name.

Deities: Information on an eclectic mix of the coordinating deities of the day.

Magical Plants & Flowers: Flowers, herbs, and plants that share the same astrological significance of the featured day. Doses of daily garden witchery and herbal spells, including flower fascinations and natural magic.

Colors, Candles & Crystals: What colors you can wear to help unify the day's energies. Spell candles to burn, and magical candle aromatherapy. Harmonizing crystals to wear, carry in your pocket, or

group around a candle. A complementary color and crystal spell or two.

Tarot Card Associations: Got a tarot deck and want to use it for more than the occasional reading? Try using certain coordinating cards as props and to focus on while you perform your spells and charms. You'll be amazed at how well they work!

Custom-Made Daily Magics: A potpourri of magical information, a smidgen of foods and bewitching spices: tips and tricks on how to take all of the information that is presented and inspire you to begin creating your own rituals and personalized magics. How to put all of the information together, plus even more theme spells and charms for the day.

If you are wondering where to find all of the various scented and colorful candles that are mentioned throughout this book, try taking a look at the little votive candle. Votives come in an impressive array of colors and scents. They are inexpensive and have a very high oil content, which means their wonderful and magical scents are released immediately as they are burned. If you have ever burned a votive candle, you will have noticed that they turn to liquid wax right away—which is why you should always burn votives inside of a votive cup, otherwise you'll get a big puddle of wax all over your work area. Check them out for yourself. Votives are a great, affordable candle to use in your own custom-made magics.

Enchantments for Every Day

These daily spells or minirituals, if you prefer, should signify something important to you. In fact, spells, charms, and rituals can be used for many purposes—connecting to deity, encouraging love, or increasing prosperity. Try performing magic for protection and healing, or to boost your creativity. The magic may take only a few moments, or it may take a bit longer. It's up to you. Now, if you're wondering how these daily spells and magics really work, I have some thoughts on that. To begin with, performing a spell can help us to focus on the sacred, and it actually slows us down.

As we begin to work our magic, our minds shift to a calm and centered place. As we go through the process of setting up for the spell, it often forces us to concentrate on the task at hand. This helps to bring us into a calmer, more focused attitude. That quiet focus is heightened when you add a little personal power and connect with deity. Then the magic that we perform helps us to concentrate on the present, while at the same time it allows us to deal with any past problems. And, finally, it encourages us to visualize our future in a more positive, life-affirming way. Most witches and other magic users will agree that there are several elements to the good performance of a ritual or a meaningful spell. Check out this list below, you'll get the idea.

The Elements of Spellwork and Ritual

Purpose: This is the purpose of the ritual. Are you focused? Did you take a moment to ground and center and to put aside all negativity? Is your intention pure? Are you sincere?

Sequence: Every ritual has a clear beginning and end. Write up a quick outline. You may find it helpful to refer to page 187, where a Daily Spell Worksheet has been provided for you. This will help you sort things out, set things up, and get ready to go.

Sacred Space: Spells and rituals cause a change in consciousness, as they take place outside of ordinary life. Toss a pretty scarf or piece of fabric over a card table. Try using the kitchen table, or be bohemian and sit on the floor. You may care to work your daily magic in a special spot, such as your altar or household shrine. Perhaps you'll want to set up in the garden or on the patio. Wherever you choose to work your magic, make it a sacred space—by this I mean a clean, happy, and pleasant environment.

Supplies: Most rituals employ complementary colored candles, herbs, crystals, and other props. You will find lots of information in each of the daily chapters that will harmonize with that day's specific magical energy. All of the correspondences and featured magical components will work in tune with each other, as they have the same sort of energy or vibration.

Why Daily Correspondences Are Important

When you add complementary natural items such as coordinating crystals, candles, magical herbs, flowers, and color to your daily spells and charms, you can increase the effectiveness of your magic. How, you may ask? Well, these items will help link your Witchcraft together with that day's magical energies. A good example of this is the power of color.

Every day of the week has its own specific magical colors. This practical type of magic should never be underestimated, even by the more experienced witch. If you select a color that harmonizes with your personal energies or goals for the day, then you will flourish.

As you begin to focus on daily magical correspondences, you will realize that the simple use of crystals, flowers, and colors can not only positively influence your personality, but your thoughts and life as well. These daily correspondences and coordinating natural items can actually strengthen the punch of the charm. They will allow you more creative ways to personalize your Witchcraft, and they will help to unify your spellwork.

A Word on the Daily Deities

As to the deity listings in this book, these will be an eclectic mix of gods and goddesses from all over the world and from many magical cultures. Now, I am aware that this idea will cause some traditionalists to clutch their chests in horror . . . hence the term *eclectic*. So what if you're calling on a Greek sun god and a Celtic goddess of light? If they are both solar deities, then they wouldn't really be incompatible. They are merely different representations of the same type of solar energy from separate magical cultures.

Come on, folks . . . relax. The best way to learn something new is to experiment and have a little fun. The planet will not stop revolving just because you mixed pantheons. The world is wide and the sky's the limit when it comes to finding a friendly deity. The gods and goddesses are many; mix and match as you like.

Advancing Your Magical Skills

The trick to advancing your magical expertise is to create your own magic. Many practitioners loudly complain about a lack of advanced techniques or materials, which always makes me wonder if they have ever considered studying, experimenting, and creating their own individual advanced magics. Maybe your specialty is working with the crystals and the stones, or you enjoy herbal spells and charms. Perhaps you're an adept at the tarot, or you have a real knack for working the candles . . .

Well, now is the time to find out where your talents lie! Listen to your instincts. Use your imagination and follow your heart. No one knows your tastes and preferences better than you do. So take a look at the magical information and correspondences presented here, use them as a starting point, and then run with it.

Are You Psyched? Great, Let's Go!

So with that thought in mind, wouldn't it be fun to have a book that you could just flip open, on any day, and find inspiring ideas, magical correspondences, deity information, quick charms, natural magic, and spells that would coordinate for that specific day of the week?

Well, my friend, look no further. Let's start talking about *7 Days of Magic*. These seven days of the bewitching week are filled with all kinds of earthy enchantments, practical magic, and witchy wisdom. Let's get your creative juices flowing! The motivation you need to craft your own magic might be only a page or two away. So pick a day, any day, and let's get started!

ॐ

SEVEN DAYS OF MAGIC

Seven are the days of the magical week,
Look inside this book for the secrets they keep.
Success, prosperity, love, and strength they hold,
To uncover their meanings, one must be bold.
Let us begin our journey, one day at a time,
May your magic be strong and true, come rain or shine.

Sunday

I

At-a-Glance Correspondences

planetary influence	Sun
planetary symbol	☉
deities	Helios, Brigid
flowers & plants	carnation, marigold, St. John's wort, sunflower
metal	gold
colors	gold, yellow, yellow-orange, neon shades of orange and yellow, hot pink
crystals & stones	carnelian, diamond, amber, tiger's-eye, quartz crystal
tarot card associations	The Sun, Ace of Wands, The Chariot
foods, herbs & spices	orange, cinnamon

Daily Magical Applications

Sunday, our first day of the week, received its name from the Latin words *Dies Solis* ("sun's day"). In ancient Greek it was called *Hemera Heliou*. In the Old English language it was known as *Sunnandaeg*; in Middle English, *Sonenday*. All of these titles mean the same thing, the "day of the sun."

What do you think of when you feel the sun shine down on you? What sorts of enchantments and energies do you think would be complementary to a day named after our closest star? Sunday brings those bright, solar energies into your life and has the magical correspondences of success, promotion, leadership, pride, light, warmth, fitness, and personal growth.

The charms and spells that would complement this magical day of the sun are ones for personal achievements of any kind—like if you are seeking fame and wealth, working for that much-deserved promotion at work, or being acknowledged for a job well done. Health issues, increasing personal power, or simply sticking to your diet and being proud of what you have accomplished—all of these goals fall under the golden influence of the sun.

———————— ☽ ————————

Deities

Getting to know more about the various pantheons and assorted deities helps you figure out whom to call on and when. Learning more about the assorted deities helps you specialize your magic. In other words, you go to specific gods for particular needs. Why is specializing so important? Well, you wouldn't call a plumber if you needed your fuse box repaired, would you? Here is a bit of information on some of the deities associated with light, success, and the sun.

There are many mythological connections between the sun and a male deity. These gods of light and fire sometimes seem to be direct contrasts to the more feminine powers of the night, water, and the moon. However, there are goddesses of light, fire, and the hearth flame as well. In truth, if you take a good look at various mythologies, you can typically find something for everyone.

HELIOS

Do you feel that you need the extra drive, ambition, and power of the God of the Sun, who sees all and watches over us as he blazes through the sky? Try picturing a buff, chariot-driving, golden-haired centurion—that would be Helios, the Greek god of the sun.

Helios was thought of as the physical representation of sun. He was portrayed as sometimes wearing a golden helmet or having a golden halo. He was often characterized in art as a handsome man draped in a white, sparkling tunic and cloak. Helios drove his blazing sun-chariot across the sky from east to west, every day. The golden chariot was pulled by his four white horses, named Pyrois, Eos, Aethon, and

Phiegon. Symbols for this sun god include the chariot, the rooster, the globe, and his four white horses.

BRIGID

The Celtic goddess of the hearth and flame, Brigid, is a triple goddess of light, inspiration, and healing. She is often associated with smithcraft, well-being, and poetry. There are many variations on the name Brigid, including Breed, Brigit, Brighid, and Brigitania. The goddess Brigid was also known as the "Bright One" or the "Bright Arrow." Often depicted as a woman with long, braided, red-gold hair, this beloved goddess of the Celts once had a sacred fire that was tended in Kildare, Ireland. In medieval times, abbey nuns tended the perpetual flame. In ancient times, it was Brigid's priestesses. Recently Brigid's flame was relit. This goddess of Erin (Ireland) will always bring illumination to hose who seek her out.

Brigid keeps the home fires burning. She is the guardian of the hearth and the goddess of flame, light, and the sun. If you have a fireplace in your home, Brigid is the deity to guard or ward it. On my mantle there is a framed picture of the triple Brigid. She watches over the home and wards our wood-burning stove and the surrounding hearth. No fireplace? Well, then, the kitchen stove is the next logical choice. Try setting out a little arrangement of three white pillar candles. Keep them lit when you are home, and watch them set an enchanting mood. You could devote them to Brigid by carving a triskele (⛥) on the sides of the candles. Those burning candles bring to mind the sacred, perpetual flame at Kildare.

Some other magical symbols for Brigid include a cauldron, as Brigid was thought to have been the keeper of the cauldron of inspiration. Another less-known symbol for Brigid is the shamrock, which could be another symbol for those candles if you have trouble carving a neat triskele. The shamrock, or three-leaf clover, was thought to represent the triple aspect of this goddess in olden times.

Magical Plants & Flowers

MARIGOLD

The common garden marigold (*Tagetes*) is a powerful little magical flower. While its scent is strong and maybe unpleasant to some folks, don't turn your nose up at it! According to folklore, it was thought that if you gathered marigolds at noon it would double their solar energy. The marigold is used to encourage wealth and riches. It also helps keeps wandering spirits away. By the way, the pot marigold (*Calendula officinalis*) is edible, and its flower petals may be added to salads or used as garnish.

ST. JOHN'S WORT

The herb St. John's wort is a perennial herb, blooming typically once a year right around Midsummer. Its magical properties include health and happiness. Try gathering the blossoms for a good luck charm, or work with the green foliage and tuck it into a vase with other magical flowers for its protective qualities.

CARNATION

The carnation is one of my favorite flowers. As cut flowers, they are inexpensive to purchase and you can even grow a miniature variety of them in the garden quite easily from seed. The carnation's spicy aroma is uplifting and healing. Try working with yellow- and orange-colored carnations to give your Sunday flower fascinations an extra boost of color magic.

A flower fascination is a simple floral type of magic that usually only employs a flower or two. The term *fascination* is defined as "to bewitch or to hold spellbound by an irresistible power." Therefore, a *flower fascination* is simply the act of working spells with magical flowers.

SUNFLOWER

The sunflower, while very easy to grow in the home garden, may only bloom for a few summer months out of the year—typically late June throughout September. However, these days it is available to us year round. The sunflower is a very popular flower in the florist's trade. So, if you don't have any blooming in the garden at the moment, pop into your local florist and pick up an inexpensive stem or two for Sunday spells.

GARDEN WITCH TIP

Here is a practical tip for working with fresh flowers. If you'd like your flowers to stay fresher in the vase for a longer period of time, then give the bottom of the stems a fresh diagonal cut with a knife or a scissors just before you plunk them into a water-filled vase. Also, strip off any lower leaves from the stems that may be below the water line. (The only thing you want in the water is the stems.) Change your water every other day and the flowers will stay fresher longer. Adding a bit of white soda, such as 7-Up, to the water is rumored to keep flowers fresher longer, too.

A Sunflower Spell

In the language of flowers, the sunflower symbolizes "high hopes and adoration." If you've ever grown sunflowers in the garden, then you have noticed how they turn their faces toward the sun throughout the day. These sun-worshipping flowers are perfect for you if you are looking to stand out in a crowd or are seeking fame and riches.

If possible, work this flower fascination outside. Set a sunflower or two into a vase full of clean water. (If you work with the flowers from the garden you may have to arrange those thick stems in something more substantial, like a decorative metal bucket or heavy vase, so the weight of the stems won't tip the vase over.) At the third line of the spell (below), turn to face the sun. Close your eyes and tip your face up to its light. Remember, while working your way to the recognition, promotion, or raise that you so richly deserve, to be fair and not to step on anyone else while you climb that ladder of success. Repeat the following spell three times:

> *I will stand head and shoulders above the crowd,*
> *I call for wealth and fame, I'll shout it out loud!*
> *Like a sunflower I turn to face the bright sun,*
> *Grant me power and triumph, and let it harm none.*

Close the spell by saying,

> *For the good of all, with harm to none,*
> *By blossom and leaf, this spell is done.*

Put them in a spot where you can see them every day to remind you of the flower fascination. Enjoy the sunflowers until they begin to fade. When it's time to dispose of them, do it neatly. Recycle them by adding them to a compost pile.

Colors, Candles & Crystals

COLORS

Colors for the day can include all shades of yellow, yellow-orange, and metallic gold. Actually, the associated metal for Sunday is gold. If you have any gold jewelry, such as a ring, a pair of earrings, a necklace—or even a fun and funky piece of costume jewelry shaped like a sun (such as a pin or pendant)—today is the day to wear it and to enchant it. Hold the jewelry up to the sunlight and ask for the energies of the day to imbue it with wealth, purpose, and achievement. Try asking Helios to bless it with drive and ambition, or ask Brigid to strengthen it with her light and divine inspiration. Then you can wear the sun-charmed jewelry any time that you feel the need for a little extra sunshine, warmth, and success.

If you care to coordinate your outfit with the bright energies of the sun, then try a shirt, blouse, scarf, or add an accessory in any of these warm colors. If you're feeling really adventurous, try the bright colors of hot pink, neon orange, and neon yellow.

A Colorful Sunny Day Spell

Try working this spell on a gloomy, rainy Sunday, or any day. It will lift your spirits, no matter what the weather.

Slip on your sunny outfit or wear your sun-theme jewelry and then take a moment to imagine yourself either on a sun-drenched beach or in the middle of a bright meadow with the sun streaming down on you. Now picture that a little of the sun's warmth is soaking into the bright colors/jewelry that you are wearing. Do you feel a bit warmer? While you are visualizing this for a moment or two, repeat the following spell three times:

Even though the skies may be cloudy and gray,

I will wear the colors of the sun today.

For the colors of yellow, gold, and orange, you see,

Work their own sunny magic, so mote it be!

Close the spell by saying,

For the good of all, with harm to none,

By color and light, this spell is done!

Then take a deep breath, blow it out, and go dazzle 'em today!

CANDLES

Candle colors for today include yellow and gold. In magic, the color yellow is used to aid communication, knowledge, and creativity. The color gold represents royalty, the God, riches, wealth, and fame. For centuries candles have been lit to welcome deity and to symbolize a connection to the magical realms. In actuality a burning candle is a physical symbol of your spell. Watch for gold metallic tapers and pillar candles around the winter holidays, you can usually pick them up on sale. Yellow may be harder to find, so keep your eyes peeled. For my candle magic, I like to work with scented votives. They come in all colors and lots of yummy fragrances. Try looking for citrus scents to bring health, and cinnamon scents for success and prosperity. These bewitching scents will help link your solar magics together with a little Sunday magical aromatherapy.

CRYSTALS

The crystals and stones associated with the sun are carnelian, tiger's-eye, quartz crystal, amber, and diamond. As stated earlier, the bewitching metal for today is gold. Gold is intimately linked to the sun's energies. It is associated with sun gods and goddesses and a majestic or regal type of energy. Gold has the powers of health, wisdom, prosperity, and success. Wearing gold jewelry will increase your personal power and give a boost to your self-confidence. It is also thought to guarantee a long life.

> *Carnelian:* The carnelian has the elemental associations of fire. It encourages protection, courage, healing, and sexuality. In ancient Egypt, rings of carnelian were worn to calm anger and to remove jealousy and hatred.

Tiger's-eye: The tiger's-eye is a fun tumbled stone to keep around. It too is associated with the element of fire and encourages protection, bravery, and good luck. Tiger's-eye also promotes prosperity and personal protection.

Quartz crystal: The quartz crystal is a powerful stone. Basically, a quartz crystal point is an amplifier. It amplifies and multiplies the powers of any other stones that it is in contact with. Quartz crystals are often used to top wands, and there is good reason for that. The crystal also amplifies your personal power.

Amber: Amber is associated with the goddess Freya. This Norse goddess of love and sexuality will be featured in Friday's chapter. Amber is associated with the sun and all of the qualities that you would come to expect: healing, strength, fame, power, and success. Amber jewelry is traditionally worn by High Priestesses and is a popular magical "stone" (it's actually a resin).

Diamond: Beyond being "a girl's best friend," the diamond promotes spirituality and self-confidence. Due to the way that the stone flashes when direct light hits it, it is also considered a protective stone. If you own any diamond jewelry, no matter what the size, it falls under the category of an associated stone of the sun.

A great way to empower any type of crystal or stone is to have the sun give them a little zap of energy. Similar to empowering your golden jewelry, hold the crystals or tumbling stones in the palms of your hands. Then lift your hands up toward the sun for a moment or two, quietly giving them a little shot of the sun's might and magic. (Try the sunny beach or meadow visualization if it will help.) Slip the tumbling stones in your pocket, or place them around a spell candle, and you're ready to go.

Sunday Crystal Spell for Success

If you enjoy working with crystals, try this natural magic spell for ambition and success. Look over the spell carefully before performing it. Either set up this spell outside or facing a sunny window. Opportune times of the day to work this sunny spell are sunrise and noon.

Gather one each of the following: a small piece of amber, a tiger's-eye tumbled stone, and a quartz crystal point. With a safe, flat surface to set up on, place a yellow candle and a candleholder in the center, and arrange the stones in a ring around the candle. Have a lighter or matches handy to light the candle.

Speak the following spell three times:

> *Around a yellow candle I create a ring,*
> *Choose tiger's-eye, amber, and quartz, it's just the thing.*
> *I call the god Helios for drive and success,*
> *Today's ambitions and career goals he will bless.*

Close the spell by saying,

For the good of all, with harm to none,
By the sun and stones, this spell is done.

Allow the candle to burn out on its own. Please remember not to leave your burning candle unattended. Pocket the sun-kissed stones and keep them with you, in your pocket or purse, for a week.

Tarot Card Associations

The tarot cards that are linked to the fiery energy of the sun's day are the Ace of Wands (or Rods or Staves) for power and clout; the Major Arcana card the Sun, which symbolizes both joy and attainment; and another Major Arcana card, the Chariot, which signifies ambition, the drive to succeed, and the willpower to overcome any obstacles in your path.

> *Ace of Wands* is associated with the element of fire. This card is a nice visual boost to job and career spells. In fact, the suit of wands or rods typically represents both your career and business life. This card in particular corresponds to successful career and business savvy, so work with this tarot symbol for help in obtaining your goals and ambitions.

> *The Sun* symbolizes joy and personal achievement. This is the card to work with on a Sunday. Its imagery is perfect for all of the magic that is associated with a Sunday. It can be used to help you focus on high ideals, and may help encourage you to be strong while you pursue your ambitions. This card traditionally portrays a young blond child riding a white horse while the sun shines down upon him. The white horse is a traditional symbol of the sun, just like Helios' four white steeds. Work with this card to bring joy, enthusiasm, and movement into your life.

ACE OF STAVES

XIX THE SUN

VII THE CHARIOT

The Chariot is a great card to work with when personal goals of any kind are the concern. This card often portrays a chariot driver who controls the direction of his path without the use of reins. In other words, he is guiding his course by the strength of his willpower alone. The Chariot card often appears in a tarot reading when a challenge of some kind must be faced. It is a powerful symbol of strength and determination. This card symbolizes a person who will succeed no matter what obstacles they face or how many unexpected curves they may encounter on life's road.

An Evaluation/Promotion Tarot Spell

Got an evaluation coming up at work? There is nothing worse than having to go over a review form. You know you deserve a good raise, but how much will your manager or the company be willing to dole out? Or are you trying for a promotion? Sounds like it's time to hedge your bets, so to speak. Try your hand at this tarot spell.

Gather the following: a yellow or gold candle (white will do in a pinch, it's an all-purpose color); our three featured tarot cards, the Ace of Wands, the Sun, and the Chariot; and an item in sympathy with the spell that you are casting.

What exactly is an item of sympathy? It is any item that is sympathetic to what you are working for. Since this is a job-related spell, an item in sympathy could be your recent paycheck stub, ID badge, or your business card. So, with that thought in mind, adding this sympathetic item to your other correspondences only helps to unify the magic. It does this by uniting the energies and giving you something very specific to focus on.

Arrange your items in front of the candle. Light the candle and focus on the cards and your item of sympathy and then repeat the spell below three times. Check out the last line of the spell and adjust this as necessary.

Just like the golden child who rides under the sun,

I call for recognition of a job well done.

Goddess, bless my ambitions, they are fair and true,

While this higher career goal/promotion I do now pursue.

Close the spell by saying,

For the good of all, with harm to none,

By the sun and stars, this spell is done.

Let the candle burn until it goes out on its own. Keep the cards and your item of sympathy together and on your person.

Custom-Made Daily Magics

Here is where we take everything that you have learned in this chapter and help you tie all of the Sunday correspondences together. If you are still confused, think of correspondences this way. Choosing complementary correspondences are not unlike selecting the ingredients for a batch of homemade chocolate-chip cookies. If you add a little chopped nuts to the cookie batter or an extra splash of vanilla, you get a more deluxe version of an otherwise basic cookie.

Now, if you were to throw something like carrots into the recipe for chocolate-chip cookie dough, that wouldn't even complement the other ingredients, would it? Nope. It would just be uncomplementary, weird, and make for a very unappetizing final product.

The reason for this cookie-spell analogy? Well, spells and charms are not unlike recipes. With a spell, you gather your ingredients, mix them together, and work the complementary ingredients for the desired outcome. So, learning how to correctly work with daily magical correspondences is a clever way to jazz up an otherwise basic or elementary spell.

With that thought in mind, here are a few more Sunday spells for you to consider.

Fitness and Health Spell

There is more to life than just climbing the ladder of success—how about personal goals, like going on a diet or beginning an exercise program or promising to live a healthier lifestyle? How about promising to take a walk a couple of times a week? These goals, too, fall under the magical associations of the sun.

For this fitness spell you will once again need an item in sympathy with your goal. If that is weight loss, then add a photo of yourself or a tiny lock of your hair. If your personal goal is to eat more healthily, as in more fruits and veggies or if you're trying to avoid sweets, then add an orange, which is another natural symbol for the sun. Quarter the orange and arrange it on a small plate. Set up a small yellow candle with your item of sympathy to the side. Repeat the following spell three times and when you are finished with the spell, eat the orange for a healthy snack.

> On this magical day of the bright golden sun,
> Now grant me the willpower to get this job done.
> I am healthier and stronger, this much is true,
> Lord and Lady, protect me in all that I do.

Close the spell by saying,

> In no way will this spell reverse or place upon me any curse. ★

★This closing line was written by a famous British witch named Sybil Leek. This is a great little all-purpose rider to close out any spell.

Sunday Sunrise Spell

Here is a spell that invokes the aid of the triple goddess Brigid. This spell is meant to warm you up from the inside out. This will cause you to have a magical sparkle and for your lovely personality to shine right through. If you don't feel particularly lovely at the moment, then maybe it's time for a change. This should help you to improve your outlook and cheer you up. Brigid is probably one of the more popular goddesses that modern witches work with—I think it is because she is so welcoming, strong, and feminine, all at once.

For this spell try working outside at sunrise. You can also beef this up by adding some natural correspondences, such as stones or flowers, to the spoken verse to help tie the energy together. You could include tiger's-eye, amber, and carnelian tumbling stones. Set these around your candles. Slip a few stems of a sun-associated flower into a vase. Try draping the workspace with a gold-colored cloth—celestial fabrics that feature bright yellow suns would be a smart choice. Or just set up in view of a sunny window and let the sunshine illuminate the workspace naturally. Repeat the spell below three times.

Sunday starts off the week with its bright golden glow,
This day brings fame, wealth, and causes friendships to grow.
Light a gold and yellow candle to ensure success,
I call on the goddess Brigid, my spell she will bless.

Her light glows inside me, from within my soul will shine,
Leadership, health, and growth will all appear in good time.

Close the spell by saying,

With all the power of three times three,
As I will it, then so shall it be.

You can work this spell whenever you feel the need for a little extra personal power. As before, you may keep the stones in your pocket for a few days. Or tuck the flowers from the spell into your hair or pin it onto your jacket like a tiny corsage. This will ensure that you carry a bit of Brigid's magic throughout your day.

*N*ow, take all of the information that you have absorbed from this chapter and add it to spells that you perform on a Sunday. When you decide to sit down and work out how to write and then cast your own spells, refer to the information that was presented in this chapter and create your own personalized magics. Refer to the various spells and charms and adapt them to suit your needs. Check out the worksheet on page 187. Make a few copies of it and get to work!

Those ambitious, successful spells and charms will be heightened by working on the day of the week that has the planetary influence of the sun. So, light those sunny candles, wear some luminous colors, and break out the gold jewelry! Bake up some cinnamon rolls for a enchanting breakfast. Take an orange with you and eat it at lunch today. Try using a little magical aromatherapy and burn some cinnamon-scented incense to encourage success and wealth today. Sprinkle some dried marigold petals around your house—or across the threshold—to pull triumph and protection toward you and your family.

Get outside and tip up your face to the sun. Acknowledge the power of Helios as he blazes across the sky and brings courage and motivation into your life. Sit outside at sunrise on a Sunday morning and bask in its warm, rosy-golden glow. Acknowledge Brigid as the inner creative spark of imagination and inspiration. She can help these gifts burn brightly within your own soul. Use your imagination and create your own brand of magic . . . here comes the sun and it's your turn to shine!

Monday

The moon shines bright:
in such a night as this . . .

Shakespeare

27

At-a-Glance Correspondences

planetary influence	Moon
planetary symbol	☽
deities	Thoth, Selene
flowers & plants	bluebell, jasmine, gardenia, white rose, white poppy, moonflower
metal	silver
colors	white, silver, pale blue
crystals & stones	moonstone, pearl
tarot card associations	The Moon, The High Priestess
foods, herbs & spices	melons, chamomile, wintergreen

Daily Magical Applications

Monday is named after the moon. The Latin term for Monday is *Dies Lunae* ("moon's day"); in the Old English language this day was *Monandaeg*; in Greek it was *Hermera Selenes*. All of these different names translate to the same thing: the "day of the moon."

Working with the different phases of the moon is an important skill that takes a bit of time for witches to learn. So why not cut to the chase and experiment with the day of the week that is dedicated to the moon in all of its magical energies and aspects?

Magically, Monday encourages the lunar energies of inspiration, illusion, prophetic dreams, emotions, psychic abilities, travel, womens' mysteries, and fertility.

Deities

Typically when folks talk about deities associated with the moon, the Goddess in her three aspects of Maiden, Mother, and Crone comes to mind. The Triple Moon Goddess is a basic principle of Wiccan belief. Understanding and working with this trinity of goddesses is often a starting point for folks that are new to the Craft. These three different aspects of the Goddess correspond to the various lunar phases, such as the Maiden for the new to waxing moon, the Mother for the full moon phase, and the Crone for the waning to the dark of the moon. One of the better-known trinity of goddesses is the classic Greek trio of Artemis the Maiden, Selene the Mother, and Hecate the Crone.

However, there are a few male gods of the moon as well. And why not, I ask you? What's wrong with a little equal time for the God? Let's not forget that the balance of male-female energies, or partnership of the God and Goddess, is an important part of our belief system as well.

While researching this moon god topic I came across some information about a horse-riding Japanese god of the moon named Tsuki-Yomi and a little-known Baltic god named Meness. Wow, these were new ones for me. Meness is a Latvian fertility moon god and was depicted as a young man wearing a star-covered silver cloak. He is crowned with stars and journeys in a chariot that is drawn across the heavens by a gray horse. I sort of like the idea of him silently swooping across the night sky, keeping an eye on us. Meness was known as a protector of travelers and a patron of soldiers. The most well-known moon god, though, is probably the Egyptian god

Thoth. He was worshiped throughout the Early Dynastic period and then into Roman times.

THOTH

Thoth, the ibis-headed god from Egypt, wore on his head both a crescent and a lunar disk. Thoth was believed to have regulated the seasons and to have helped keep the lunar phases on track. He was regarded as a magus, the greatest of all magicians. Thoth was a fair and benevolent god of wisdom, astronomy, and practical skills, and he presided over education and books. He was a patron deity of the scribes and his protection included written medical and mathematical knowledge. Thoth had a wife named Sheshat, and her title was Mistress of the House of Books. Sheshat was a goddess of writing, stars, books, history, and invention. She was depicted as a woman with a star on her brow who wore an inverted or horns-down crescent moon on her forehead.

SELENE

Selene is a Greek goddess of the full moon. She is often portrayed within the face of the full moon as a beautiful, winged woman wearing a golden crown. There are Homeric hymns dedicated to Selene, as she was a very influential goddess of her time. One of the lines gives a romantic description of the goddess: "From her golden crown the dim air is made to glitter as her rays turn night to noon." The final section of the hymn reads, "Her great orbit is full and as she waxes a most brilliant light appears in the sky. Thus to mortals she is a sign and a token."

Selene is a favorite goddess of modern witches. Why? Well, her specialties include helping you find practical, commonsense answers to your problems. Solutions appear quickly within a day or so. When you call on Selene, you basically get broom-side assistance. Now, before someone starts imagining a dramatic *flash-boom!* accompanied by a swirl of fairy dust, hang on for a second . . .

Selene sends her practical solutions quietly and in unexpected ways. Plus, best of all, spells and prayers dedicated to Selene get results almost every time. However, if you don't pay attention, you may miss the magic. Selene is subtle. Watch closely and see how she sends in her magical assistance in a practical, no-nonsense fashion. Symbols for Selene include white flowers, the bluebell, and, of course, the moon.

Magical Plants & Flowers

BLUEBELL

Bluebells are linked to the moon because of the tale of Selene and her handsome lover Endymion. The botanical name for bluebells is *Endymion nonscriptus*. Selene could not bear the thought of losing him to old age and death so she cast a spell on her lover, thereby keeping him eternally handsome and youthful. Her lover sleeps away eternity with a smile, while Selene visits him in his dreams. As she visits Endymion, the moon wanes to dark. When Selene returns to her duties once again, the moon waxes to full. Mythology states that Selene bore Endymion fifty beautiful but sleepy daughters. Is it any wonder that he is always smiling? On an interesting final note, in the language of flowers the bluebell means "constancy." Adding blue-bells to a love or romance spell will gain special attention from Selene.

JASMINE

Jasmine is a flowering vine that has an extraordinary scent. In magical herbalism, the delicate jasmine bloom is associated with the moon. The jasmine flowers were thought to promote prophetic dreams and to help encourage a spiritual love.

GARDENIA

Another scented lunar flower, the gardenia is a popular, creamy-white bridal flower that encourages love and mysticism.

WHITE ROSE

The white rose is a sacred symbol to many goddesses. A full blown, or opened, white rose is a symbol of Selene, the full moon goddess. The white rose traditionally symbolized purity and love.

WHITE POPPY

The white poppy, another of Selene's sacred plants, is also an enchanting flower. On an amusing note, in the language of flowers it symbolizes "drifting in a peaceful sleep." (No wonder Selene claimed it!)

MOONFLOWER

The moonflower is an annual flowering vine. Part of the morning glory family, *Impomea* moonflowers have an intoxicating scent. And, just as you would imagine, they only bloom at night. Moonflowers are a natural when it comes to working a little Monday night moon magic. Try gathering a bloom and floating it in a bowl of water. I often float a bloom in my small garden fountain in the backyard. Or leave the blooms on the vine and work your spell while you sit nearby and enjoy the fragrance.

A Moonflower Dream Spell

Traditionally the moonflower carries the message of "I am sustained by your affections," just like Endymion was sustained by Selene's love. Try this moonflower-inspired spell and send your lover a sweet dream of you.

Gather from the garden a white rose, a single moonflower blossom, or any of the lunar-associated flowers that were mentioned above. Float the bloom in a fountain or a birdbath, or use a clear glass bowl. If you use a bowl, hold the bowl in your hands and concentrate on the lunar symbolism, both of the round, moon-shaped, circular bowl and the white flower floating within. If you use a fountain, then adapt this accordingly. Close your eyes and gently concentrate on your partner. Picture in your mind a happy time or future event that you are both looking forward to. Open your eyes and repeat the following spell three times.

> *My love, while you sleep I will send you a sweet dream,*
> *By the light of the moon, things are not as they seem.*
> *I cast upon the water petals from a white flower,*
> *May Selene now bless my spell in this enchanted hour.*

Close the spell by saying,

> *For the good of all, with harm to none,*
> *By moonlight and dreams, this spell is done.*

Note: Be sure to leave the theme of the dream up to the dreamer. You are "suggesting" only, not manipulating the outcome or coercing their private thoughts. This spell also works well when your partner is having trouble sleeping and you want to encourage a restful night's sleep. Brew up a cup of chamomile tea and set it next to the candles. When you are finished with the spell, quickly give the tea to your partner and wish them a "good night." It should work like a charm.

Colors, Candles & Crystals

COLORS

Colors for this lunar day may include white, silver, and pale blue or gray. The associated metal for Monday is silver. Silver is a receptive metal and is identified with the lunar energies of the goddess. Silver is the metal of emotions, magic, psychic abilities, and of peace. Charging or empowering silver jewelry works along the same lines as the directions that were given in Sunday's chapter for enchanting gold jewelry, the main difference being that you want to work in the moonlight as opposed to the sunlight. This time hold the jewelry up to the light of the moon and ask either Selene to enchant it or Thoth to imbue it with wisdom and knowledge.

If you want to feel a little more witchy on Mondays, then try adding a little color magic to your outfit by adding those lunar colors that were listed earlier. Any soft, shimmery fabrics in delicate lunar colors would work out nicely as well. Add a silver pin shaped like a moon and you're all set and ready to go!

Lunar Illusion Color Magic Spell

Feel the need to blend in or to go about your business quietly, without drawing attention to yourself? There are times when we all need to be, well . . . a little subtle. Now, before you get in a huff at what I am suggesting, think about it for a moment. Sometimes even those of us who are naturally outgoing need to tone things down a bit—like when you have had an argument with your mother, or you are approaching your boss about an issue at work, or taking on one of your kid's teachers at school. There are times when it is simply not appropriate to swagger into situations with your six guns a'blazing.

For those times when discretion, tact, and a little magical strategy is called for, this lunar illusion spell will help to keep you centered and calm. If you need to work magic discreetly, or for those times when being subtly witchy is the way to go, this sort of quietly clever magical control goes a long way in situations when tempers are frayed and emotions are high. This glamoury-type of enchantment is particularly useful when you want to win people over to your side, or for when you are quietly working magic to smooth over sticky situations.

Choose your outfit with care. Think of quiet, lunar types of colors or silver jewelry. No matter what your personal style is, whether you slip on a gray business suit, tug on a white sweater, or pull on a comfortable denim shirt in a soft blue, this lunar illusion will work. Take a moment and imagine yourself standing on the quiet, moonlit shores of a lake. Feel yourself becoming serene and filled with the power and magic of the moon. Now, wrap a little of the moon's light and glamour around you. Do you feel more centered and focused? Good. Now believe that you can calmly and quietly handle this situation. Repeat the spell below three times.

The lunar shades of magic are white, silver, and blue,
Charm, mystique, and illusion they grant softly to you.

Peace and serenity are the order of the day,
May this spell smooth all obstacles that are in my way.

Close the spell by saying,

For the good of all, with harm to none,
With color and light, this spell is done!

Take a deep breath, and let it out slowly. Now, coolly go and deal with the crisis.

Note: Remember, this spell works to smooth situations over, not to eliminate them. In other words, you can glide in, fix the situation, and then quietly ease back out. It also makes people see you in a different light, so be ethical and make sure you use this spell fairly.

CANDLES

Candle colors for today include white, silver, and pale blue. Keep your eyes open for celestial-themed candles with moons and stars on them. Try your hand at a little candle-magic aromatherapy. All of the following fragrances are associated with the moon: gardenia-scented candles promote spirituality and love; jasmine-scented candles encourage peace, sleep, and psychic dreams; sandalwood, a highly spiritual scent, may be used to support meditation and helps to set an excellent magical mood. All of these enchanting fragrances correspond to Monday and the moon with its gentle magic.

CRYSTALS

The crystals and stones that are linked to the moon are the quartz crystal, moonstone, pearl, and sapphire. Moonstones and quartz crystals can easily be purchased at nature-theme stores or at most magic or metaphysical shops. These tumbled stones are typically inexpensive, so pick up a couple of your favorites and keep them on hand for crystal magic and spells.

Quartz crystal: Extra power for any charm, and it's all-purpose.

Moonstone: Moon magic, safe travel, psychic powers, gardening, a goddess stone.

Pearl: A moon symbol, women's magic, good fortune, and fertility.

Sapphire: Protection, sorcery, and healing. It will also increase your psychic abilities.

You may care to enchant these lunar stones by placing them on a windowsill that receives the moonlight, or setting them in a dish and leaving them in the garden on the night of a full moon, letting them soak up some lunar energy. If you own any pearl or sapphire jewelry, then let them stay indoors on a moonlit windowsill. (I wouldn't recommend leaving your good jewelry outdoors overnight.)

Since traditionally the moonstone was used as a talisman to promote safe travel, let's conjure up a moonstone travel spell.

Moonstone Travel Spell

This spell will call on Meness, the patron moon god of travelers. Set up this spell in the evening. Find a spot that faces east or that is illuminated by moonlight. Or try setting this up in the garden under the moon. Try using a scented candle, as previously suggested, to coordinate with the energies of the moon.

Gather the following items: four small tumbled moonstones; a white candle and holder (try a tealight candle in an old glass jar or a pretty holder); a safe, flat surface to burn the candle on; and a lighter or matches.

Light the candle and place it in the holder. Arrange the four stones in a circle around the holder. Repeat the following spell three times:

Meness, patron of travelers, watch over me,

Whether I travel in the air, on land, or sea.

Like a talisman, in my pocket a stone will I tuck,

Moonstones do encourage a safe journey and bring good luck.

Take one of the stones and keep it in your pocket while you travel. You may close the spell by saying,

For the good of all, with harm to none,
By the moon and stars, this spell is done.

Allow the candle to burn out on its own. If you performed this outside, then move your candle indoors to let it safely finish burning.

Tarot Card Associations

The tarot cards that are associated with the moon's day are the Major Arcana cards the Moon, which symbolizes illusion, and the High Priestess (or Popess), which means intuition, dreams, and magical powers.

The Moon is an intriguing tarot card. Often this card is interpreted as a time of disillusionment or despair, but not always. This card is a symbol for the Crone Goddess and it also signifies illusion and a development of psychic powers. This is the card to work with and meditate on when you feel that there are hidden forces at work or where you may not be seeing things as they really are—you know, the new boyfriend who seems too good to be true? The boss who seems to have a hidden agenda? You get the idea.

The High Priestess symbolizes wisdom, mystery, feminine power, and magics. This card typically represents the Goddess in her aspect as the Maiden. This card is the one to work with when you want to increase and call on your inner natural magical powers. We all have our own magic. Dig deep and see if you can call it out. If you want to learn how to be more empathic and tune in to your natural psychic abilities (and everybody has those, too, by the way), this is the card to meditate on and to focus on in your spellwork.

XVIII THE MOON

II THE POPESS

44

Increasing Psychic Powers Tarot Spell

Feel like working for a little increased intuition or psychic ability? Here is a Monday night tarot spell that will help you increase your psychic talents and focus on your own powers.

This spell will incorporate many of the bewitching accessories that were mentioned earlier in this chapter, such as candles, aromatherapy, and crystals. For this tarot spell, I would probably go with a scented white candle. Try jasmine or sandalwood for this spell, as both are equated with the moon and they are spiritual scents that help encourage intuition and empathy. Arrange the Moon and the High Priestess cards on either side of the candle. Add a few moonstones or a quartz crystal to this spell. Also have some silver star confetti or glitter available. These moon-associated crystals are known to increase psychic abilities.

Make the work area pretty and magical. Try adding a silvery or shimmery piece of cloth to drape over the area. Prop the cards up so you can focus on them during the spell. Arrange the other accessories in a way that pleases you and take a moment to center yourself. Repeat the spell below three times. On the last line, sprinkle a bit of celestial or silver star-shaped confetti in a circle going clockwise around you.

I call upon the Lady to open my heart
In olden times prophecy was the witches' art.
Clear sight, empathy, and intuition now bring,

In all seasons, fall to winter, summer to spring.
By the powers of water, fire, earth, and wind,
With stardust and moonlight may my visions begin.

Now, sit inside of the circle that you just cast on the ground with the confetti and allow your mind to drift. Let your intuition take over. Lay out a quick tarot spread and see what the cards have to tell you about the current situation. A very simple card spread to use is just to deal out three cards: one for the past, one for the present, and the final card to represent to future. Meditate on the cards for a moment or two. Close the spell by saying,

As I close this spell, I bring harm to none
By moonlight and magic, my spell is done.
In no way will this spell reverse or place upon me any curse.

You may either let the candle burn until it goes out on its own or pinch it out and save it to use when you do a tarot card reading at a later time. If you start to experience vivid dreams, then start a dream journal and keep track of them. Pay attention to your "gut hunches" and start listening to your inner voice. Everyone has psychic abilities of some sort. Don't deny any psychic experiences that you have, no matter how small they may seem. Instead, write down your experiences and validate them. You receive more psychic impressions and you begin to become more comfortable with your own intuition when you begin to acknowledge the experiences instead of brushing them off.

Custom-Made Daily Magics

Here are a few more moon-associated spells for you to try your hand at. The first spell calls on Thoth, the Egyptian god of wisdom and magic. If you wish to try and "beef up" your magical prowess, so to speak, then working with Thoth is the way to go. As Thoth was considered the greatest of all magicians and a benevolent god to boot, he should be able to help you cleverly increase your powers and help you to gain a little magical wisdom while you are at it.

The Spell of the Magus

Try working this spell on a Monday while both the moon and the sun are in the sky at the same time. During certain phases of the waning moon, the moon can be seen in the morning sky or in the new to waxing moon phase in the evening sky just before the sun sets. This time when both the sun and the moon are visible in the sky is believed to be a time of incredible magical power.

Light a white candle and place it in a candleholder on a safe, flat surface. Gather a few almonds in a dish off to the side of the candleholder. Almonds are sacred to Thoth, and are thought to grant wisdom. **Note:** If you are allergic to nuts then substitute with a white wintergreen-flavored mint. Wintergreen is also associated with the moon.

Repeat the spell below three times.

Thoth, Egyptian god of wisdom and of the moon so white,
Hear my call, grant me might and power on this special night.
Honor and integrity creates its own power,
Grant me wisdom and strength in this magical hour.

At the final repetition of the spell, eat the almonds or, alternatively, the mint, then close the spell by saying,

As I consume these nuts / this mint, I take into myself
the wisdom and benevolence of Thoth.
For the good of all, with harm to none,
By the moon and stars, this spell is done.

Keep an eye on the candle; let it burn until it goes out on its own. Meditate on the old saying that with great power comes great responsibility. Be sure you are fair and wise in all of your magical actions. If you are unsure of your motives, then contemplate Thoth, use your imagination, and see what he has to tell you.

Selene's Spell

This last spell calls on Selene, our featured lunar goddess of practical magic and commonsense solutions. Look over the spell before you begin, as you will need a few supplies. This spell is also a good one to work on the night of a full moon, no matter what day of the week it is. Simply adjust the opening line—try saying instead, "On the night of Selene's enchanted full moon"—and you're good to go. Happy casting!

Gather the following: one white taper candle; one silver taper candle; two candleholders; a white rose in a vase; matches or a lighter; sandalwood incense and a incense holder. Have a safe, flat surface on which to set up the spell.

Set up this spell so you can see the moon, no matter what phase she is in. Light the candles and the incense. Center yourself and repeat the spell below three times.

> *Monday is the magical day of the moon,*
> *In this enchanted time, hear this witch's tune.*
> *See the white and silver candles burning so bright,*
> *I call the goddess Selene for her help this night.*
> *Practical solutions are her shining gifts, you see.*
> *Lady, show me the way, as I will, so mote it be.*

Close the spell by saying,

Selene, I thank you for your time and care,

I close this spell now by the powers of earth, water, fire, and air.

Again, you may save these candles to use on the full moon or any time you call on Selene. Enjoy the rose until it starts to fade, then carefully gather the petals and spread them out to dry in a single layer. After they have dried, store them in an airtight nonporous container. (Old glass canning jars are ideal for this purpose.) Then use those enchanted petals in spells where you need to "speed things up." Keep your eyes open and see how Selene's power and your moon magic goes to work in your life.

Think for a moment on all of the magics and enchantments that you discovered in this moon-themed chapter. Don't be afraid to adjust these spells to suit your own specific needs. Also, there is that handy-dandy spell worksheet on page 187 for you to copy and work on.

These gentle, illusory, and dreamy charms and spells can be enhanced when you work on the day of the week that is dedicated to the moon. Light up those lunar scented candles and add a little mystique to your outfit by wearing an enchanting lunar color. Wear your sparkling silver jewelry and maybe add a pair of dangling silver earrings shaped like crescent moons. Burn some sandalwood or jasmine-scented incense today to inspire the glamour and magic of the moon. Slice up a favorite variety of melon for a snack or share it with your love and enjoy his or her lunar and romantic qualities. Brew up a cup of chamomile tea, enchant it with a little moon magic, and relax and get a good night's sleep.

Most importantly, get outside tonight and watch the moon for a while. What phase is she in? What color was the moon as she rose? Why not start a journal and note down where the moon rises for a few seasons? This is a great way to teach you to tune in and to become more aware of the moon and the influence that she pulls into our lives. Try calling on Selene for her magical assistance, and call Thoth for wisdom and strength. Be imaginative and create your own personal lunar magics. Go on . . . the moonlight becomes you.

Tuesday

Seize the day!

Horace

53

At-a-Glance Correspondences

planetary influence	Mars
planetary symbol	♂
deities	Mars, Lilith
flowers & plants	holly, snapdragon, thistle
metal	iron
colors	red, black, scarlet, orange
crystals & stones	bloodstone, garnet, ruby
tarot card associations	Five of Wands, Six of Wands, Strength
foods, herbs & spices	allspice, peppers, carrots, garlic, ginger

Daily Magical Applications

Tuesday is a Mars day. Mars was the Roman god of war. If you're wondering how this day came to be named, it's because to the Germanic people, this day became Tiw's day (Tuesday). Tuesday actually got its name from the Norse deity Tyr, Tiw, or Tiu, also a god of war. This deity was very similar to the Roman Mars, and the days of the week became switched and substituted as the Germanic peoples replaced the older deities with their own gods. So the name was changed from the Latin *Dies Martis* ("Mars' day") to the Old English *Tiwesdaeg*.

The Norse god Tiw was a patron of athletes and sporting events. He was known for his sense of justice, discipline, and integrity. This day's planetary influence brings with it the aggression, bravery, and honor of soldiers, as well as the passion and strength of those of us who must fight for what we believe in.

Deities

MARS

Mars may have been originally a god of vegetation, but as time went on he became more closely linked to Ares, the Greek god of war. Mars was one of the major deities of the Roman pantheon. Like his Norse counterpart Tiw, he was a patron god of soldiers and was often portrayed as wearing a cape, a suit of armor, and a plumed helmet. Mars' symbols can include a shield and a spear. It is believed that the month of March got its name from the Roman god Mars, in part due to the violent swings in the weather, not unlike Mars' temperament.

LILITH

Lilith is the divine lady owl and the original bad-ass chick. She is often portrayed as a dark, winged, beguiling sorceress. Our most familiar image of Lilith comes from a terra cotta relief from Sumer, dating back to about 2000 BCE. She is shown as an attractive winged woman with clawed feet. In modern times, she is popularly imagined as the beautiful vampire and the ultimate femme fatale. It is easy to envision Lilith as a raven-haired seductress draped in flowing black, her ebony wings swirling around her. She is thought to be ethereally beautiful, with pale skin, dark red lips, and perhaps a small flash of elongated teeth. Seductive, aggressive, and dangerous—Lilith is all of these things.

To modern practitioners, Lilith is a patroness of witches and a goddess of sexuality, wisdom, female equality, power, and independence. While Lilith is not traditionally linked to a Tuesday, I don't see why we couldn't work with her on this day.

Tuesday

Perhaps it's time to make some new traditions. Sometimes you gotta go with your gut—personalize your magics! Go with what you think will work best for you. After all, Lilith's feisty and fiery qualities are perfect for a Tuesday. These aggressive and strong characteristics are just what is called for.

Magical Plants & Flowers

A few of the plants associated with Mars and Tuesdays are the thistle, holly, and the snapdragon. Now, if you think about it, two of these plants have "prickles" on them. Thistles can have very prickly stems, and the leaves of the holly typically have sharp, pointy ends. The snapdragon, a favorite cottage-style flower of mine, has the elemental association of fire and is also aligned with Mars. All of these magical plants are utilized for their protective and fiery qualities. This trio of magical plants is often worked into hex-breaking and defensive magic.

However, before you start running around in a panic, worrying about someone trying to zap you with a naughty spell, relax. In actuality, a hex is a very rare occurrence. These Mars-associated plants will help to shield you from your average manipulation, and that occurs more often than anything else. Manipulation is not always a magical problem, sometimes it's an everyday one—from the coworker who cons you into doing their job for them, or from the well-meaning in-laws who think that if they just apply enough pressure, then, *perhaps*, you will fall in line, to the person or partner who thinks they can just walk all over you because you always give in. These are the manipulation problems you are much more likely to face.

So, just because these plants have the ability to break a hex or to stop evil doesn't mean that you will have to use them for that on a regular basis. Mars plants tend to be protective plants and when you apply a little practical magic and common sense with their magical qualities, you get an unbeatable combination.

THISTLE

According to folklore, when thistles are allowed to grow in the garden it is thought to protect the home from burglary. Thistles grown in containers by the front or back door are supposed to have the power to ward off evil and negativity. If you feel the need to break up any negative energy or manipulative intentions that you believe may have been sent your way, then thistle is the plant to work with. Thistle is a wild-flower and often volunteers in the garden. If you have a sunny spot well out of the way of young children, who need to watch out for the thorny leaves and prickly stems, consider letting it grow wild.

HOLLY

The holly (*Ilex*) comes in many varieties and species. Not all hollies bear fruit (in other words, berries). The female holly will produce the berries, while the male produces small greenish flowers for pollination and a few berries. One male holly will pollinate many female hollies. Check with your neighbors and see if they have a male variety; if not, you will have to pick one up so they can pollinate, and the female holly will then produce lots of pretty berries for you. The holly has the charming folk name of "bat's wings." If you take a good look at most modern varieties of holly, you can see how those leaves look a bit like the shape of a bat's wing.

When the holly shrub is grown in the garden, it is thought to protect the home from lightning and roguish magicians. If you feel that you might have fallen under the crossfire of a less-than-ethical practitioner, a problematic coworker, or (more likely) a meddling relative, then try adding holly leaves to your spellwork.

SNAPDRAGON

Snapdragons are a great magical flower. They grow happily in most gardens and thrive in containers. If you pinch off the flowering tops after they fade, they will keep blooming for you all season long. Snaps have the elemental association of fire and they are a very protective flower. Snapdragons can break any manipulative intentions or bad mojo that might be tossed your way. Try a little flower magic on those problematic relatives or nosy neighbors and give them a small container planted full of red snapdragons. That should help to break the animosity between the two of you. As a cut flower, snapdragons are available at most florists year-round and come in many colors. Try red for protection and yellow for wisdom. Look for orange colors for energy and passion.

If you feel the need for a little reinforced protection at work, then arrange a couple of stems of snapdragons in a vase and set them on your desk. Not only will the flowers perk you up, but they create a sort of no-fly zone around you. Then other people's head games and office dramas will pass you right by. If you are not allowed to have flowers at work, try picking up a few packages of snapdragon seeds this spring. Tuck a package of the seeds in your desk or, if things are really bad, then try discreetly sprinkling just a few seeds across the troublemaker's desk or on their office floor, where they will be sure to walk on them.

The Warrior Spell

Let's combine these magical protective and fiery plants for a kick-ass flower fascination. Hey, it's a Mars day, after all! Everybody has a bad day or goes through trying times. Life can throw you a curve and then you find your-self in the middle of a painful situation. Before you know it, your self-con-fidence is shot, and you feel victimized and wonder how in the world this ever happened. When tough situations come your way, concentrate on Mars' warrior-like and feisty qualities. Then take a deep breath and let go of your fear.

As you prepare to work this spell, take a good look at what you are so worried about or afraid of. Give yourself some time and deal with your emotions. If you find yourself shedding a few tears, it's no big deal. You probably needed the release that only a good cry can bring. (So what if your nose is red? It's a Mars color, after all.) Take a few minutes and concentrate on being braver, stronger, and able to handle anything that life tosses your way. Remember, you are not a victim! Turn that fear into an ally and chan-nel that energy into protection instead. Take this as an opportunity to be brave and strong and to deal with the problem. Now, blow your nose, wash your face, and take a deep breath. Be a calm and powerful magical warrior! You can do it, I know you can.

Gather from the garden three stems of snapdragons (red, if possible), a stem or two of blooming thistle, and nine holly leaves. Combining these three plants will invoke protection and encourage passion and bravery. If you cannot locate a live thistle, then consider looking for dried thistle at a herb shop or at the arts and crafts store. As for the snapdragons, you can always go to the florist if they are out of season, or during the spring and summer months purchase a six pack of the annual to add to your magical gardens. Then the flowers are available for your flower spells and to enjoy.

Arrange the flowers in a water-filled bud vase and then position the holly leaves in a circle around that. Add a red ribbon to your flowers to help reinforce both the magic of a Tuesday and Mars' fiery qualities. Take a red ink pen and a piece of paper and write down the challenge that you are facing. Set this list under the vase and within the circle of the holly leaves. Ground and center yourself. Let go of your anger and put your game face on. Now, repeat the spell below three times.

> *Mars' fiery energy now encircle me,*
> *A witch is a warrior, I set my fears free.*
> *Purple thistle, holly leaves, and snapdragons three,*
> *Passion, courage, and bravery now send to me!*
> *I release all my worries, they have no more power,*
> *This warrior's spell is cast, by leaf and by flower.*

Close the spell by saying,

> *For the good of all, with harm to none,*
> *By herb and thorn, this spell is now done!*

Let the flowers stay in the vase for a few days until they begin to fade. Then gather up the components from this spell and tuck the holly leaves and flowers into an envelope. Seal it, then tie the red ribbon around the envelope and take it right out and into the garbage. Drop it in and brush off your hands. Slap the lid on the can and strut away.

So, do you feel more confident? Good. Now put all this garbage behind you. People only have the power to hurt you when you let them. Next time you have to see or deal with them, be confident, be friendly, and give them a cocky smile. That ought to confuse the hell out of them. Rise above and conquer!

Colors, Candles & Crystals

COLORS

Colors for the day include red, black, scarlet, and orange. The metal associated with Tuesday is iron. Got any black wrought-iron candleholders? These would coordinate with your Tuesday magic quite nicely. Black is for boundaries and fighting negativity; it's great for protection spells. Scarlet is a daring, passionate hue that adds *oomph* to candle spells. Orange is used in spells for energy, courage, vitality, and charisma.

The color red is considered by many Asian cultures to be a lucky and sacred color. Red is believed to promote power, strength, and fame, and is, of course, associated with the element of fire. In China, it is traditional for a bride's gown to be red; also, a proud father of a newborn son will hand out red eggs. It is also thought that wearing red ribbons will direct and retain positive *chi*, or energy.

If you care to coordinate your outfit with the warrior energy of the day, then try adding a cherry-red scarf or blouse. Ladies, you may want to wear red lipstick or crimson-hued lingerie. Guys might want to go with a red sweater or a fiery-colored tie. If you're a casual sort of person, then try sporting a red t-shirt, sweatshirt, or even bright red socks!

CANDLES

Candle colors for today include all shades of red, from oranges to scarlet to deep burgundy. Also, try working with black candles to absorb negativity and to break bad luck. If you want to add a little magical candle aromatherapy, then go for spicy or coffee-scented candles. Believe it or not, the aroma of coffee is an energy booster. It

sharpens your other senses and if you overdo it on the aromatherapy and you can't smell anything anymore, then taking a whiff of coffee beans can actually refresh your sense of smell!

Here is another little tip. Look for carrot-cake scented candles. (No, I am not kidding.) Carrots and spices are both associated with Mars and the spicy scent of the candle corresponds with Tuesday and all of its passionate, daring qualities.

Hot Stuff Candle Spell

Want to drive your lover crazy? This candle spell is meant to entice and tempt—the whole point of it is to add a little spark back into your relationship and to make you irresistible. Please remember to be conscientious of this spell and only work this upon yourself, so you and your partner can have a little fun.

Gather a red candle, a black candle, and two candleholders. Sprinkle a dash of pepper and a pinch of allspice on the unlit candles. Arrange three snapdragons or three red roses in a vase. Repeat the following charm three times:

As I light red and black candles for a hot and sexy spell,
I now call on Lilith for passion and all will be well.
Peppers and spice and snapdragons / red roses three,
These will make me very enticing, so now must it be.

Close the spell with,

For the good of all, with harm to none,
May my love and I have a little fun!

Now, go and find your lover, give him or her a bewitching smile, and see what kind of reaction you get.

CRYSTALS

The crystals and stones that are linked to Tuesday's fiery, passionate energy are garnet, bloodstone, and ruby. While two of these fall under the gemstone category, you can find low-grade rubies as a tumbled stone. (I picked one up for about a dollar.) It works out nicely in my Mars-themed spells. Since these stones all fall under the elemental correspondence of fire, then you may choose to empower them by passing them above a candle flame or by letting them sit in the sun's rays for a short while.

Garnet: The garnet is thought to enhance your strength and endurance. Once this stone was used to frighten away criminals, spooks, and ghosts. It can help to strengthen your aura and may help to give off a "don't mess with me" type of vibe.

Bloodstone: One of my favorite stones, the bloodstone is a beautiful, deep green stone called chalcedony that is flecked with deep red. The next time you are at a shop that sells inexpensive tumbled stones, sort through the bloodstones and find one that "speaks" to you. Hold the stone in your receptive hand (opposite from the one that you write with) and then see if you notice anything. When you find one that gives you a little zap, makes your palm tingle, or makes you feel warmer, you will know you've found a keeper.

Ruby: The ruby is a stone of love, power, and wealth. When rubies are worn, they increase personal protection. Rubies can help relieve sadness and they reinforce a healing, positive outlook.

Red Jasper: The red jasper is a great stone to utilize in protective and defensive magics. It encourages healing and is used in beauty-enhancement spells. Women can charm jasper beads or tumbled stones to boost their appearance—sort of a very earthy type of glamour.

A Bloodstone Protection and Courage Spell

The bloodstone, when worn or carried, brings courage and eliminates fear and anger. The bloodstone was often used as a talisman for athletes and warriors. When you need a little extra courage and bravery to face challenges and stressful, scary situations, give this practical witch's spell a whirl.

For this particular crystal spell, you will need a few supplies: a red spicy-scented votive candle, a votive candle cup, three bloodstones (use inexpensive tumbled stones, these are perfect), a photo of yourself or a small snip of your own hair, a small cast-iron cauldron, and matches or a lighter. Set up on a safe, flat surface.

Place the photo or snip of hair in the bottom of the cauldron. Now place the candle inside of the holder. Set this in the center of the small cauldron, on top of the photo or the hair. (If you are worried about the heat damaging the photo, then set the photo beneath the cauldron.) Next, arrange the three bloodstones around the candleholder. Ground and center yourself. Then, when you are ready, light the candle and repeat the following spell three times:

On this Mars day, there is fiery energy to spare,
I call for courage and passion to know, to will, to dare!
Three green bloodstones and a burning candle of red,
I call for bravery and banish fear and dread.

Focus on the flame for a few moments. Believe in your ability to handle the situation, whatever it may be.

Close the spell by saying,

For the good of all, with harm to none,

By Mars' energy, this spell is done.

Let the candle burn until it is consumed. If this is an ongoing problem or conflict, then repeat the spell every day for one week. (In other words, from a Tuesday until the following Tuesday.) Clean out the votive cup and light a new red votive candle for each day of the spell. When you are finished working this, clean up your setup and put all of the components from this spell away. If you like, you can carry those tumbled bloodstones with you to help reinforce your convictions.

Tarot Card Associations

The tarot cards that align with Tuesday and Mars energies are the Six of Wands, for victory and triumph; the Five of Wands, which symbolizes the ability to handle life's little annoyances; and the Major Arcana card Strength (or Fortitude), which, oddly enough, stands for inner strength and self-control.

The tarot suit of Wands (or Rods or Staves, depending on your deck) is associated with the element of fire. The element of fire coordinates with the warrior-type planetary energies of Mars and Tuesday's passionate and feisty qualities. The suit of Wands is for folks who are fighters, dreamers, and rebels. The featured tarot cards in this chapter are both powerful and passionate symbols, so use them wisely.

Six of Wands is often interpreted as a card of victory. This card often shows up in tarot readings when your hard work is finally being recognized, or when you feel as if you have just won a major battle of some kind in your life. This card makes a great prop in magic. It gives you a very specific image of victory to focus on, and the image of a victorious rider helps to encourage the movement and energy that you want to promote with your spellwork.

Five of Wands is an intriguing card. At first when folks see this card they see struggles and conflicts. What they often miss is that this card usually signifies a person who enjoys dealing with minor problems and day-to-day obstacles. This person loves to get in there and set things right again. You know, the type of personality who you imagine as "kicking

butt and taking names"? This is their card. This person adores challenges and revels in the excitement that only a good argument or debate can bring. This card encourages excitement and helps you to "step up" and face the average problems that life often throws your way.

Strength is usually depicted in one of two ways. It may show (depending on your deck) Hercules battling a lion or a woman who embraces a lion and holds the lion's head gently within her arms. This card stands for self-control and the ability to handle things during a crisis by tapping into your inner strength. This is the card of quiet strength, conviction, gentle courage, heroism, and valor.

Here is a tarot card spell for you to try. This spell comes in handy during those stressful times of your life when you need a little extra courage and strength.

Victory Through Strength Tarot Spell

This tarot spell may be set up simply or more elaborately; it is up to you. Don't be afraid to make your magic personal and unique.

Either use the featured cards (Six of Wands, Five of Wands, and Strength) as your only props around a red candle or add the associated crystals for a Tuesday (ruby, bloodstone, and garnet). Try draping the workspace with a red cloth or scarf. Consider working this spell at sunrise or at noon, when the sun is directly overhead and bright. I suggest setting the candle and its holder in the center of your workspace, then arranging the cards and other accessories around it.

Another good idea would be to scatter those flat-bottomed, red glass marbles on the work surface. (You know, those pretty glass gems that are so popular for wedding-reception table decorations?) You can pick up a bag of those at most arts and crafts stores for a few bucks. Find some iridescent ones, wouldn't they look sharp? Use your imagination! How about holly leaves or red flower petals? Are you getting inspired yet? Good. Now psych yourself up and repeat the spell below three times.

The lady holds the lion within her arms,

My strength comes from my soul and causes no harm.

I hold the power to succeed time and time again,

Honor and victory are mine, let the spell begin.

Meditate on the symbolism of the cards for a short time. Close the spell by saying,

For the good of all, causing harm to none,

By fire and passion, this spell is done!

Let the candle burn until it goes out on its own. If you used stones in the spell, you may keep them with you for a few days in your purse or pocket to help reinforce the spell.

Custom-Made Daily Magics

Now that you are starting to get into the passionate, courageous, and daring qualities of Tuesday, here are a few more spells for you to experiment with. Don't be afraid to adapt these spells to suit your needs. As long as your intentions are honorable, I am sure they will work out beautifully.

The "Enchanted Evening" Elemental Spell

Looking to put a little passion back into your love life? How do you feel about working with the four elements and Lilith, our goddess of power and passion? There are times when even the most loving relationship needs a little *oomph*. So, if you simply want to spice things up with your partner in the bedroom . . . well, hey, Lilith's your best bet! But be careful. She has a wicked sense of humor. Calling on Lilith for some extra spark or desire works very well and you may feel like you have a magical hangover in the morning. A small price to pay . . . just don't say that I didn't warn you.

Let's get all of your senses involved. This spell is a sensual and sensory experience. To represent the four elements in this spell, light a few black or red candles to represent the element of fire. Burn dragon's blood incense to represent the element of air. To symbolize water, open a bottle of red wine and drink from the same cup as your partner. Finally, sprinkle the sheets with some crimson-colored rose petals to represent the element of earth.

And at the risk of sounding like a mom, don't forget while you're setting this stage for loving seduction to practice safe sex! Ask for Lilith's blessings by using the following invocation:

Lilith, dark goddess, teach me to love, laugh, and be wise,

Aid me in my witchery as you sail through the skies.

By the natural magics of air, water, earth, and fire,

I manifest the gifts of love, seduction, and desire.

By the elements four, this spell is now begun,

As I will, so shall it be, and let it harm none.

Mars' Energy Spell

Try your hand at this fiery spell for courage, passion, and winning battles. Incorporate as many warm Mars-like colors as you can into it.

Set a few tumbled stones next to a candleholder containing a red or an orange candle—try a ruby for power and a red jasper to encourage protection and defending yourself. Work with those pretty red glass marbles again. Also, try adding a bit of spice to this one. Toss a pinch of garlic in the candleholder to promote protection. Try adding a pinch of allspice to bring good fortune and success. Set the candle on top of these spices and you're all set. Repeat the following spell three times:

Tuesday is the day for fiery, aggressive Mars,
Live with courage and passion and you will go far.
Candle colors for today are bright orange and red,
These will draw success and deflect all harm and dread.
Help me to win my battles fairly, both great and small
While I show kindness and compassion to one and all.

Close the spell by saying,

By all the power of three times three,
As I will it, then so shall it be.

Let the candle burn until it is consumed. Make sure you have it in a safe place to finish burning.

Tuesday is the day to work any magics that fall in the category of increasing strength, courage, bravery, and passion. All of these intense emotions are linked to this day's energies, and spells designed around these themes will have extra punch when performed on this magical day.

So, let's add a little passion and conviction into your life! Break out the daring red pieces of your wardrobe and put a little pizazz into your day. Try working with a little aromatherapy and burn some spicy or coffee-scented candles to increase your energy level.

Create some kitchen magic and whip up a spicy stew—add in a few Mars-associated ingredients, such as carrots, peppers, and garlic. Empower the stew for success and then treat yourself and your family to a good, hearty meal.

Check the sky at night and see if you can find the reddish planet Mars up in the heavens. Not sure where to look? Check an astronomy magazine or search the Web for more information.

Become a magical warrior and move forward in your life with strength, courage, and compassion. Embrace the side of yourself that loves a good challenge and that is passionate and daring! Believe in yourself and in your dreams, and you will win every time.

Wednesday

*E*very smile makes you
a day younger.
Chinese Proverb

79

At-a-Glance Correspondences

planetary influence	Mercury
planetary symbol	☿
deities	Mercury/Hermes, Odin, Athena
flowers & plants	fern, lavender, lily of the valley, aspen tree
metal	quicksilver
colors	purple, orange
crystals & stones	opal, agate, aventurine
tarot card associations	Wheel of Fortune, The Magician, Eight of Pentacles
foods, herbs & spices	dill, lavender

Daily Magical Applications

To the Romans, this day was called *Dies Mercurii*, or "Mercury's Day." Mercury was a popular character in the Roman pantheon—a messenger of the gods, he presided over commerce, trade, and anything that required skill or dexterity. The Celts also worshiped Mercury, and eventually equated him with the Norse god Odin (some spelling variations on this name include Wotan, Woden, and Wodan). Odin, one of the main gods in Norse mythology, was constantly seeking wisdom. He travelled the world in disguise as a one-eyed man with a long, grey beard, wearing an old, beat-up hat and carrying a staff. (Which brings to my mind images of Gandalf from *The Lord of the Rings*.) In the Old English language, this day of Mercury evolved into *Wodnes-daeg*, "Woden's day," or Wednesday.

Wednesday carries all of the magical energies and associations of this witty and nimble god himself. Some of these traits included good communication skills, cleverness, intelligence, creativity, business sense, writing, artistic talent, trickiness, and thievery. And don't forget all of those wise and enigmatic qualities associated with our Norse pal Woden, not to mention the goddess Athena's contributions of music, the arts, handmade crafts, and writing. Wednesdays are great for seeking wisdom and for improving your skills, be they in trade and commerce, music and art, or in communication and writing.

——————— ☽ ———————

Deities

MERCURY/HERMES

Mercury is the fleet-footed Roman god of commerce, travel, self-expression, speed, and science. Mercury had a sacred festival day called the Mercuralia, and that was held in Rome on May 15. To the Greeks he was known as Hermes, and his symbols included winged sandals or boots and a winged cap of invisibility. There is a theory that the cap he wears can be a symbol for secrets and concealed feelings or thoughts. Mercury/Hermes also carried a bag full of magic, and he held a magical healing rod with two intertwined, winged serpents called the caduceus.

While Mercury's caduceus was a symbol of heralds and commerce, the caduceus of Hermes became linked with medicine sometime during the seventh century BCE. As Hermes became linked with alchemy, the alchemists were called "the sons of Hermes." These practitioners of the Hermetic arts were also known as Hermeticists. Both Mercury and Hermes are known as the god "with the winged feet."

This is a god of the crossroads, a guardian of commerce and anything that requires skill and dexterity. Mercury/Hermes is a multifaceted god and one of contradictions. He was also known as a patron deity of thieves for his sneaky, tricky, and cunning attributes. (According to mythology, as an infant he stole the god Apollo's cattle.) On the flip side of the coin, he can be both benevolent and helpful to shopkeepers and tradesmen as a god of profit and a guardian of merchants. This is a god of unexpected luck, happy coincidences, and synchronicity.

A familiar icon today, this Greco-Roman god is famous as the golden emblem for a major floral delivery service that advertises speedy and efficient floral delivery

worldwide. Remember, Mercury/Hermes was known as a joker and a clever and cunning magician. And I'll just bet you that old Mercury or Hermes is secretly tickled at all of the attention that he still unknowingly receives from florists every day of the year.

ODIN

A Norse god of wisdom and poetry, Odin hung on the World Tree, Yggdraisil, for nine days, seeking power. He gained several songs of power and twenty-four runes. Odin carried a spear that never missed its target. Trading one of his eyes for a drink from the well of wisdom, his sacrifice gained him immense knowledge. Odin was a god of mystery and magic who also became wrapped up in the mythology of Mercury, and was called by many names, including Wodin, Wotan, and Ohdinn. Odin is associated with the element of air and the horse, raven, wolf, and eagle.

ATHENA

Athena is a warrior-maiden goddess of wisdom, war, crafts, and poetry. In her war aspect she is known as Pallas Athena. Some of the more familiar symbols for Athena are the javelin, spear, shield, and plumed helmet. She was usually depicted with an owl perched on her shoulder as well, to symbolize wisdom. There is some debate over Athena's origins. Traditional mythology says that she sprang full grown and ready to rumble from her father Zeus's head, while another school of thought believes that she may have been originally a Mycenaean goddess of home and hearth.

Athena was called "bright-eyed" and was a patroness of women's rights and freedom. She also presided over craftsmen, potters, weavers, and spinners. To round things up, Athena was also associated with writing, music, wisdom, justice, and peace. In this aspect her symbols are the owl and the olive tree. In a Homeric hymn to Athena, she is described as a "glorious goddess, gray-eyed, resourceful and of implacable heart." The birthday of Athena was celebrated on March 23. Her sacred city was, of course, Athens.

———————— ∂ ————————

Magical Plants & Flowers

Let's take a quick peek at some of the enchanting plants that have the planetary association of Mercury, and that are connected with a Wednesday. For this tricky and changeable day of the week we have the fern, lavender, lily of the valley, and the aspen tree. As you'll see, some of these plants are quite easy to link with the various deity information that's already been discussed in this chapter. Just like the multifaceted god Mercury/Hermes, this bewitching day of the week and the following Mercury-aligned magical plants can cover a wide variety of magical uses.

FERN

The fern is a traditional witch's garden plant. Whether these are found growing in the wild or tucked into your backyard shade gardens, ferns are practical magical plants. The fern has quite a bit of folk history behind it. It was thought that to grow ferns in the garden was lucky. Fairies were believed to jealously guard the fern. (Ferns were thought to grant the power of invisibility, you see.) When a fern frond was carried on your person it was thought to guide the wearer to hidden riches. On an interesting note, ferns are almost always used in fresh flower arrangements. Flower folklore tells us that adding ferns to a fresh flower arrangement increases the power and meanings of the individual blossoms, and it bestows protection on the recipient.

LAVENDER

Lavender is a popular aromatherapy flower. The scent of lavender is thought to reduce headaches, and it has a healing, calming influence that soothes the spirit.

Lavender is a protective herb. This herb is associated with benevolent Witchcraft. The lavender is a shielding and healing plant. It also has the qualities of banishing negativity and keeping negative thoughtforms at bay. Lavender is a herb of transformation, so it's a perfect addition to spells and charms for Wednesday, our unpredictable, changeable day of the week.

LILY OF THE VALLEY

Lily of the valley is an old-fashioned cottage garden plant. This fragrant, romantic flower is also associated with Mercury. These lovely, scented plants are best suited for growing in the shade and will multiply rapidly if you do not keep them under control in your garden. Flower folklore warns of planting lily of the valley alone. Instead, plant other magical shade-loving flowers such as columbine or foxglove along with them, to keep the garden happy. Lily of the valley is toxic if ingested, so simply enjoy the blooms in small arrangements or just for their scent in the garden. The scent of lily of the valley was thought to have the power to improve the memory and to lift the spirits. In the language of flowers, the lily of the valley speaks of a true, platonic friendship and a return to cheerfulness and happy times.

ASPEN TREE

The aspen tree is a tree of healing. It is associated with communication and the element of air. Also, aspen leaves were often used in spells designed to protect you from thieves. Well, it's not to hard to imagine why this tree ended up being aligned with Mercury, now, is it? Remember that Mercury was associated with speed, trickiness, and healing.

The aspen tree always appears to be in perpetual motion. The slightest breeze causes the leaves to tremble and shiver. A folk name for the aspen was the "whispering tree," due to the sounds that the rustling leaves seem to make while they dance in the breeze. In the old days it was believed that the winds carried messages straight to the gods. The aspen then became associated with movement and communication, just like our pal Mercury/Hermes.

Aspen Leaf Communication Spell

Have you been trying to get a hold of someone? Perhaps it's an old friend that you haven't been able to track down, or a relative that you need to clear the air with. Perhaps it's a coworker who keeps "misplacing" your memos, messages, or notes. Then here is a clever natural-magic spell to try.

For this herbal spell you will need to gather three aspen leaves for movement and the positive reception of your message. This spell relies on the element of air and all of the qualities associated with this element, such as motion, contact, change, and intelligence. As stated above, the aspen is intimately connected with the element of air. So, unite these two enchanting energies and try a little natural magic to send your magical message quickly on its way. Remember that this spell is designed to give the recipient a friendly nudge, sort of a psychic "Hey, I really need you to give me a call" type of energy.

Gather the leaves and hold them in your hands; at the third line of the spell (below), scatter the leaves to the breeze. Or, if you would prefer, try simply working with the aspen tree by sitting on the ground, beneath its branches. Then repeat the spell three times while a nice breeze ruffles the leaves overhead.

Aspen leaves first are green and then in autumn turn to gold,
I call the element of air, for I am brave and bold.
As these aspen leaves catch the breeze, my spell to you will soar,
With the speed of Mercury and the help of the winds four.

Close the spell with the line,

For the good of all, with harm to none,
By leaf and breeze, this spell is now done!

Once you have made contact, the communication between the two of you is up to the spellcaster. But this spell should at least help you to get things moving in a positive direction.

Colors, Candles & Crystals

COLORS

There are a few different ideas for colors associated with Mercury and Wednesdays. Honestly, did you expect anything else? Some traditions say that orange is the color for Mercury, while others claim that it's purple or a mixture of colors. So guess what this means? It means that you get to decide for yourself which color you'd like to use.

Personally, I don't see anything wrong with using both purple and orange for Wednesday spells. After all, both of these colors are secondary colors. Remember your color wheel lessons from elementary school? In other words, it takes red to make each of them. Yellow and red make orange, while blue and red create purple. Are you following me here? Since both colors are produced with a base color of red, why not use them both?

If you wanted to wear the colors of this changeable and communicative day, then go with either purple or orange. If the thought of slipping on an orange shirt makes you cringe, then look for deeper shades in burnt orange or softer shades of melon to stimulate communication skills and to increase your productivity. Ladies, try looking for shades of cosmetics in coral and give that a try.

If purple is more your style, and it does seem to be a very popular color among magic users, then go for it! Whip out a deep-violet colored blouse. Slip on a deep purple tie or scarf. Maybe you have a favorite dark purple sweatshirt or casual pullover. Ladies, you can try wearing eye shadow in shades of plums and purples, or nail polish in any tone from pale lilac to deep amethyst. Mercury is a mutable sign, which means that it is constantly changing. There are many magical qualities to this day of the week. See what you can discover for yourself by working with a little Wednesday color magic.

Mercury's Colors Candle Spell

This spell reminds me of the line my two sons often throw around the house, in a deep and dramatic voice, complete with a cheesy foreign accent: "Yes, my brother, you are bold—but are you also . . . daring?" Well, are you? Are you ready to dive into the complex and varied moods and attributes of a Wednesday? I thought you might be. Give this candle spell a little whirl and see how it works out for you.

While gathering your supplies, try adding a bit of Wednesday aromatherapy while you're at it—see if you can find two lavender-scented, purple candles for this candle spell. Don't forget that lavender is a herb of transformation and magic! Other supplies you will need are two orange candles, four candleholders, matches or a lighter, and a safe, flat surface to set up on.

This spell will help you to invoke, or call on, all of the clever and skillful attributes of this magical day of the week. Expect to notice a difference within a day or so. But remember, if you are brave enough to work this spell designed to improve your communication skills, then you need to be daring enough to step up and use these gifts in a positive and productive way.   Repeat the following spell three times. Allow the candles to burn until they go out on their own.

I light purple candles for power on a Wednesday eve,
Now burn the orange candles for skill and dexterity.
From these two colors springs magic, on this fascinating day,
Send wisdom, communication skills, and clarity my way.

Close the spell with this line:

For the good of all, with harm to none,
By color and light, this spell is done!

GARDEN WITCH TIP

Lavender comes in many varieties. If it's classified as a "tender perennial," it may not survive cold winter climates. It grows best in full sun and along the edge of a sidewalk or driveway. It can be drought tolerant but you'll still have to keep it watered occasionally so it will look and flower its best. Plant plenty of this wonderful-smelling herb—it's great for sachets, dried flower arrangements, and it's a powerful magical herb that encourages the transformation of your dreams to reality.

CRYSTALS

The stones and crystals that are associated with Mercury and Wednesdays are the opal, agate, and aventurine.

Opal: The opal is a beautiful multicolored stone. It was thought that if you wrapped an opal inside of a fresh bay leaf that this would grant you the power of invisibility. I think it's much more likely that it may help you to remain unseen, or safely in the background. The opal is also thought to increase psychic powers if worn. (Scott Cunningham's *Encyclopedia of Crystal, Gem & Metal Magic* suggests wearing earrings for this purpose.) Opals make a good subtle choice for magical jewelry. They are thought to increase your self-esteem and bring out your inner beauty or "sparkle."

Agate: The agate comes in many different shades and colors. Each color has its own meaning and, in keeping with the theme of this chapter, the meanings are many and varied. Here are a few examples of different agates and their magical meanings:

Banded agate: These are protective stones. Wearing jewelry made of agates is thought to keep the wearer calm and centered.

Blue lace agate: A good de-stressing stone. Try carrying a tumbled stone in your pocket or tuck a blue lace agate into your desk drawer at work.

Brown agate: A charm for prosperity and success.

Green agate: A lucky stone for healing spells, green agate is thought to help improve the strength of your eyes.

Moss agate: A gardener's stone. If you wear moss agates they will help to restore your energy and vitality after a long day, or after you wore yourself out by working in the garden. In magic, the moss agate was used to promote luck, prosperity, and longevity.

Red agate: This is a protective and healing stone as well. Try working with this stone for health issues and to rid the body of infections.

Aventurine: This is thought of as a gambler's stone. It is also associated with Mercury and has many of the same magical attributes as that wily god. This green, inexpensive tumbled stone is perfect to carry in your purse or pocket to promote success and prosperity and to encourage good luck. The lovely green color of this stone was also believed to soothe emotional storms and help to speed up the healing process.

Wednesday All-Purpose Agate Spell

Try using tumbled stones for this spell. They are inexpensive and can be picked up at most metaphysical or magical shops. Even nature-themed stores or arts and crafts stores often carry tumbled stones. This is a great spell for a friend or loved one who is going through a tough time. This crystal spell pretty much covers all the bases. The next time a friend asks for a little magical help, you'll know just what to do.

Gather several different colors or varieties of agates (tumbled stones). I would say that about four to six different colored agates would be plenty. Ring the agates around a plain white tealight candle in a holder, and then repeat the following spell three times:

Lovely agates come in many colors and hues,

May this charm grant luck and prosperity to you.

Health, wisdom, and protection, for you now do I call,

In all seasons, winter to spring and summer to fall.

Close the spell with,

By all the powers of three times three,

As I will it, then so shall it be!

Let the tealight burn until it goes out on its own. Then give the stones as a gift to your friend and tell them to keep them in a spot where they will see them daily for a month. (Or from one full moon phase to the next.) They can either keep the agates or return them to you after the month has passed.

Tarot Card Associations

The tarot cards that are associated with Wednesdays and Mercury's attributes are the Wheel of Fortune, which represents good luck and chance events; the Magician (or Juggler) for skill, confidence, and communication; and the Eight of Pentacles (or Coins) for craftsmanship, skilled work, and pride in your accomplishments.

> *Wheel of Fortune* is a Major Arcana card that literally means "chance." This is a card of fate. It symbolizes good fortune and a unexpected twist of fate. When the Wheel of Fortune card shows up, things are bound to change, possibly for the better. This is a card of good luck and happy coincidence. This card ties in nicely to the Mercury energy of the day.

> *The Magician* is a card of power, communication, confidence, and skills. The Magician is traditionally depicted as a man standing behind an altar that holds the four magical tools—a wand, a pentacle, a cup, and a sword. One tool to represent each element. A master of the elements, one of his arms is raised while the other points downward; think of it as "As above, so below." This card characterizes a person who is quietly powerful and is confident, charming, and articulate.

> Adding this card as a prop in your spells will give you a big visual boost. Take a good look at the magical images that are represented within this card. It's called "the Magician" for a reason, you know.

> *Eight of Pentacles* is a card of the skilled craftsperson. It can represent a hobby or profession that you take pride in or a talent that you cleverly

X THE WHEEL OF FORTUNE

I THE JUGGLER

EIGHT OF COINS

use to make a little extra money. Whether it's painting, weaving, sewing, pottery, or jewelry making, this is a craft that you create with your hands. This card indicates that you get more out of your talents than just a monetary bonus (although that can't be discounted). What this symbolizes is the sense of pride and personal satisfaction that you gain from using your imagination, creating the object, and in working with your own two hands to produce something special.

A Tarot Spell to Increase Creativity

This spell is designed to give your creative juices a little boost. No matter how talented you are, everybody hits a creative wall now and then. I have two very artistic and witchy friends. One is a mother, shopkeeper, and talented artist. The other is a full-time college student and part-time jewelry designer. And from time to time they can both hit a little creative snag. Something doesn't turn out the way they intended or a project just won't gel. Do they give up? Nope, they either look at the project from a different perspective or they let creativity take over and lead them to a different outcome than they had originally planned. The results are typically stunning.

So, with this thought in mind, let's look to our goddess for Wednesday, Athena. After all, Athena was a patron of the arts and of skilled craftspeople. How about using a little tarot magic and seeing what kind of imaginative and crafty things we can come up with?

Gather the following: a table or tray to set up this spell on; a white votive candle (it's an all-purpose color); a votive cup/holder; a representation of Athena's sacred bird, the owl (try using a picture or a tiny figurine); the tarot cards the Magician, the Eight of Pentacles, and the Wheel of Fortune; a sample of your project; a few art supplies (if you are an artist, then set a couple of art pencils or paints on the workspace; if you sew, use a swatch of fabric; if you create jewelry, then set out a few beads, and so on. This is your item/items in sympathy).

Arrange your items around the candleholder. Set the tarot cards around the items of sympathy. Light the candle and repeat the following spell three times:

Gray-eyed Athena, patron of handmade crafts and the arts,
Send your divine inspiration, let it fill up my heart.
Throw in a bit of good luck and a dose of your wisdom.
Now, may my creativity take on a fresh, new spin!

Close the spell by saying,

I thank the goddess Athena for her time and care,
I close this spell by the powers of the earth, water, fire, and air.

Keep an eye on the candle. Let the candle burn until it goes out on its own (a votive candle will take about six to eight hours). Allow the items of sympathy to stay where they are for a while. Then take a little time off from your project. When the candle is consumed, take a fresh look at your project. Are you getting any new and innovative ideas? I bet you'll come up with something fabulous!

Custom-Made Daily Magics

This chapter was, without a doubt, the toughest one to write. Mercury is such a varied planetary energy and there are so many different magical qualities to a Wednesday that the subject became more than a little overwhelming. I would sit at the computer for hours and wonder where to go with this chapter. I was getting frustrated and aggravated. The harder I tried to pin this day down, the less I actually had. Then my mother rode into the rescue. She called and asked me how my new book was coming along. I laughed and told her that I was seriously considering banging my head against the computer to see if that could get me anywhere. When she suggested that I get out of the house and meet her for lunch, I pounced on the offer. She advised me that the change of scenery would probably do me a world of good.

As I drove to meet her for lunch, I was sitting at a stop light waiting for it to turn green. It was then I noticed that the car in front of me had "Mercury" on the back of it. That gave me a little jolt. As a rule, I don't pay attention to the make or model of other cars while I drive. It's a blue car or a white truck to me, that's about as technical as I get. I smiled to myself and continued to drive.

In the ten minutes it took me to drive to the restaurant where I was to meet my mother, I saw four different Mercury cars. Weird. When a floral delivery van pulled in front of me with that logo of a golden Mercury emblazoned across the side, I began to chuckle. Okay, so he was a god of synchronicity, after all. *Duh, Ellen . . . communication, changeability, and cunning.* Finally it dawned on me. Mercury was doing everything possible to get my attention.

I ended up laughing out loud. "Okay, thanks, I got it. Message received!" Mercury is a god of many faces, attributes, and guises, I reminded myself.

Maybe it was time to focus on the many varieties of magic that could be performed on this wild and wily day, as opposed to just picking one theme. So with a little help from my mom and Mercury himself, this chapter finally came to be.

To wrap up this chapter, let's work a little fun, practical magic for good luck. Try this next spell out. It will require you to go on a hunt for one of the supplies, but honestly, that's half the fun!

Quick As a Flash Spell (For Good Luck)

This good luck spell will require you to locate a Mercury dime. A Mercury or silver dime was a dime minted in the year 1940. It does not actually portray the god Mercury on the coin. What it shows is Lady Liberty in a winged cap. However, it does look like Mercury, and many folks thought that's who it was, so the name stuck. How to find them? Check a coin dealer or, if you have a family member who collects coins, see if they have one. I called a local coin shop and was told I could pick a Mercury dime up for about a dollar or so.

Occasionally, if you work retail or man the cash register, you come across silver dimes. If you look at the side of the coin the color is silver all the way through. Plus it makes a different type of "clink" as it hits the change drawer. Happy hunting!

Take yourself, a tablespoon of dill (a Mercury herb used for prosperity and luck), and your Mercury dime, and go to the nearest crossroads early on a Wednesday evening. This can be any place where two streets intersect. Also bring the spell below written on a piece of paper. Perhaps you'll want to do this while you're out walking the dog or taking a walk around the neighborhood with the kids. You can be subtle with this spell, as it is a quick one. It's not complicated and it's fun! Read the spell below softly, repeating it three times.

> *Wednesday is for Mercury, that quick and nimble god,*
> *A clever and canny soul, on winged feet he does trod.*
> *Leave a Mercury dime at the crossroads tonight,*
> *Quick as a flash, my good luck spell will now take flight.*

Slip the paper back into your pocket. Make your wish for good luck and then chuck the dime out there. (I caution you to stay away from traffic. I also don't want you to accidentally nail a car with the dime as you toss it out there into the middle of the street.) Sprinkle the dill at the curb. As you turn to walk back home, then close the spell with,

> *By all the power of three times three,*
> *As I will it, then so shall it be.*

Note: If you perform this spell and you have your kids along, let them gently toss a penny along with your dime. They'll think it's fun and that way they'll leave your dime alone. Good luck to you and yours!

Mercury is a mutable energy and its moods and associations are many and varied. Take a good look at the spell worksheet on page 187 and get to work! What do you think you can come up with to personalize your magics? When in doubt, you can always try the tarot spell for creativity on page 97. Adapt the spell as necessary to suit your needs.

Perhaps you've got a yen to write. Well, go ahead—don't let anyone stop you. Mercury days are also for communication and, after all, writing is communication. It's the writer's way of communicating with their audience. They either tell the reader a story or they teach the reader something new. (This is the part where I really hope that I have managed to teach you something new—and maybe even inspired you to write your own spells.)

Not too sure about that yet? Maybe you should sit down and have a little chat with Athena, goddess of the arts, wisdom, and peace. Don't forget that the arts include writing and music as well. Try meditating on Athena and see where that takes you. Here is a simple candle spell to help get you going.

Athena's Spell Writing Charm

Light a purple candle for Athena and a white candle for peace. Now sit before the candles and concentrate on what variety of spell you'd like to write. Close your eyes for a few moments and center yourself. Now repeat the following spell three times:

> *Computer and printer, ink pens and paper,*
> *Send me inspiration sooner than later.*
> *Athena blesses me under a Wednesday night sky.*
> *I can create my own spells, now let my magic fly!*

Close this up by writing your own spell or charm. If you'd like to add a little herbal magic to this spell, add some lavender for transformation. It will help to transform your ideas into reality. Check your spice rack, and make use of some dill for good luck. Most of all, just have fun. Don't be afraid to try writing your own spells.

*B*e bold and daring today! Expand your knowledge of the Craft by working with the energies of Mercury on his multifaceted day of the week. Create something new and work on your communication techniques. Conjure up a little good luck for yourself. Call on Athena to inspire you to try arts and crafts.

Consider Mercury/Hermes and all of the many lessons he has for you. Wednesday is the wild and wily day of the week, so try and go with the flow; don't fight the quirky energies of the day. Most importantly, follow your heart and always keep a good sense of humor.

Thursday

Would that you might pray also
in the fullness of your joy and
in the days of abundance.

Kahlil Gibran

At-a-Glance Correspondences

planetary influence	Jupiter
planetary symbol	♃
deities	Thor, Juno, Jupiter, Zeus
flowers & plants	honeysuckle, cinquefoil, mint, maple tree, oak tree
metal	tin
colors	purple, royal blue, green
crystals & stones	sapphire, amethyst, turquoise
tarot card associations	Ten of Pentacles, Nine of Pentacles, Ace of Pentacles
foods, herbs & spices	cinnamon, nutmeg, wheat

Daily Magical Applications

Thursday comes from the Latin *Dies Iovis*, which means "Jove's day." Jove, or Jupiter as he was sometimes called, was the supreme god and patron of the ancient Romans. Jove/Jupiter is associated with wealth, leadership, thunder, and lightning. A lord of heaven, Jove/Jupiter was also a god of light and his sacred color is white. In the Greek mythologies, this deity was known as Zeus.

This fifth day of our bewitching week was eventually turned into the Old English *Thursdaeg* or *Thunresdaeg*, which translates to "thunder's day" or, more simply, "Thor's day." This day of the week is named after Thor, the popular Norse god of thunder. Thor was the son of Odin. He carried a war hammer called Mjollnir, and it was this that made the thunder and lightning. All of these Thursday gods—Jupiter/Jove, Zeus, and Thor—were wielders of the thunderbolt.

Thursday has the planetary association of Jupiter, and this day of the week is associated with prosperity, abundance, leadership, and good health. Prosperity and abundance are the typical magical concerns on a Thursday. However, the way people define prosperity can vary greatly between individuals.

Personally, I think prosperity and abundance aren't about owning the biggest house, fanciest wardrobe, or the newest car. It's about living within your means, and living well. My definition of prosperity is having enough money in the checking account to cover the bills and to pay for the groceries. (With three teenagers—two of them six-foot-plus boys—the grocery bills are pretty hefty.) Anything left over is gravy.

But with a family there is always something. Just about the time you're feeling confident, something pops up. Somebody has to go to the doctor, or one of the kids needs new glasses or new shoes. Or fifty bucks for sports camp . . . oh, that's due next week, by the way. It's enough to drive you bonkers! For instance, just this week my three teenagers all lined up in the living room to announce to their father and me that they each needed thirty-five bucks for their high-school yearbooks. Ouch!

The aspiration to make your budget stretch and to find ways to cover extra expenses is a real need for just about everybody. So on this magical day, let's look at some practical, magical ways to increase your prosperity and try out a few enchanting ideas designed to create a little abundance and, last but not least, good health.

Deities

THOR

This fifth day of the week is dedicated to Thor, for he was—and is—greatly loved. People called on Thor to protect them from evil and to bless them with both fertility and abundance. Thor was pictured with red hair and a red beard, and he was thought to be hearty and hot tempered. He was married to a golden-haired goddess named Sif, and Thor was the strongest of all the Norse gods. When he used the hammer he wore a belt or girdle that could double his strength, and he wore magical iron gauntlets. When Thor rode the Earth in a chariot that was pulled by two gigantic male goats, he brought rain to germinate the crops and to make the fields fertile. The people believed that the turning of his chariot's wheels made the sound of thunder.

Even though he may seem a warlike god, Thor was not. His hammer was thought to be a symbol of the god's beneficence. The symbol was used to bless both infants and brides. (There are references to Thor blessing a bride by having her hold the hammer in her lap.) Yes, this was a macho-type god of storms and lightning; however, he was also associated with fertility and abundance. Thor is worshiped as a benevolent god, one who protected both the other gods and men from evil and destruction. Thor brought fruitfulness to the fields and happiness in marriage.

JUPITER

The Roman sky god and ruler of their pantheon, sometimes called Jove. Identified with Zeus in Greek mythology, he was also identified by the German people with their god of thunder, Thor. The Roman Jupiter/Jove was associated with hospitality (probably because he always rode herd on the squabbling Olympians) and he was also in charge of laws and social order on earth. Oaths, treaties, and alliances were sworn in his name, which led to the custom of swearing in his name "By Jupiter!" or "By Jove!"

ZEUS

The leader of the Greek gods and the head honcho of Olympus, Zeus was the god of the sky, and his weapon was the thunderbolt. He was married to Hera and was known for his weakness for the ladies. His symbols include the eagle, oak tree, and lightning bolt. Zeus's image appeared on gold coins and the sculptor Phidias carved a giant statue of Zeus made entirely of ivory and gold. This statue became one of the most famous images in ancient times, and was one of the Seven Wonders of the Ancient World.

JUNO

Juno was an ancient Roman great mother goddess. The mature and powerful Queen of Olympus, she was a powerful matriarch in her own right. Juno was a source of fertility, a goddess of marriage and childbirth, a guardian of women and children, and a goddess of money. She was known by many names, including Juno Augusta, the harvest mother; Juno Februata, the mother of Mars; and Juno Lucina, the mother of light. In this latter aspect the goddess was pictured as carrying a torch or scepter of light.

Juno was associated with the lily, the cuckoo, and the peacock. In processionals, Juno's priestesses carried fans made of peacock feathers. The many "eyes" on the feathers were thought to watch over women and they symbolized the fifty priestesses who served at Juno's temple.

To tie in with our Thursday theme of prosperity and abundance, Juno was also known as Juno Moneta. The word *money* actually comes from the word *moneta*. In ancient times, Juno's temples housed the Roman mint. Coins that were made there were considered to be blessed by the goddess herself.

Magical Plants & Flowers

HONEYSUCKLE

The foliage and flowers of the honeysuckle have long been used to promote prosperity. The scent of honeysuckle is also used to promote psychic abilities and to encourage abundance. It was thought that by bringing honeysuckle into the home, a wedding was sure to follow. This may have something to do with the old folklore behind the language of flowers. Honeysuckle represented the ties of love and a deep and generous affection.

CINQUEFOIL

Cinquefoil is also known as five-finger grass. The five points of the leaves symbolize love, riches, good health, power, and knowledge. This blooming herb is often worked into prosperity and healing spells. In the language of flowers this plant signifies a loving mother-daughter relationship.

MINT

The mint is a much-maligned garden plant. The reason for its bad reputation in the garden is that it is classified as invasive—which means it will spread like crazy! Mint (*Mentha* spp.) comes in an impressive array of varieties and scents: spearmint, apple mint, chocolate mint, peppermint . . . If you want to grow mint in the garden, then keep it corralled by planting it in pots or containers, or try sinking that container into the ground so the roots and shoots will stay under control. Magically, mint is worked into both money and health spells and charms. Add a few fresh mint leaves

to a charm bag or tuck them into your wallet to promote prosperity. Also, taking a whiff of fresh mint can alleviate nausea and is thought to refresh you and to help clear your head. Pretty cool, huh?

MAPLE TREE

The maple tree's foliage and small branches are often utilized in both love and prosperity work. If you are looking for a way to "sweeten your life up," this is both a readily available and practical magical tree to work with. Try creating a small wand out of a fallen branch and use that in your prosperity and loving abundance spells.

OAK TREE

The oak tree has a vast and colorful magical history throughout the world. The oak's planetary influence is Jupiter, and the tree is associated with the element of fire. Many magical cultures revere the oak. The oak is associated with the many sky-thunder gods, such as our featured gods Thor, Zeus, and Jupiter. Actually, the rustling of oak leaves in the breeze was thought to represent the voice of Zeus.

The foliage of the oak was celebrated as a happy, protective, and lucky symbol, and folks adorned themselves with garland of its leaves. In modern-day folk art it is common to see oak leaves in green man masks, and worked into hex signs for protection and such. The oak tree also plays a major role in the winter and summer solstice celebrations, both in the decorations and in the symbolism of the Holly King and the Oak King.

Work with oak leaves and small fallen branches for prosperity, healing, courage, and luck. Try picking up a few fallen acorns and tucking them into your pocket like talismans. (This was thought to boost your fertility as well.) If you want a small natural representation of the God to place on your altar or workplace, then try adding a few acorns or a small twig covered in oak leaves.

Oak and Maple Leaf Spell

Here is a Thursday-night spell to try. This is a quick and practical type of magic that is based on the lore and magic of the trees. As discussed before, the maple and the oak are both linked to Thursdays and to Jupiter's influences of prosperity, abundance, and good health.

Gather a few leaves from an oak and maple tree ahead of time for this spell. If you can pull it off, this would be a great spell to work while it is thundering outside—but please work this spell indoors if safety is an issue. Arrange the leaves around a green votive candle in a pretty holder. Raise up your personal power and picture yourself vibrantly healthy and your life flowing with abundance. If this is difficult for you at the moment, then do your best to lay your fears aside and to focus on the improvements that you are trying to achieve. Now, repeat the following spell three times:

I call on Thursday's thunder gods to come aid me in my plight.
Leaves of oak and maple tree I add to my spell tonight.
Oak for protection and prosperity, and for courage true,
Maple leaves for health and bounty, guard me in all that I do.

Thursday

This green candle spell brings abundance and healing galore,
With a little help from the gods Jupiter, Zeus, and Thor.

Close up the spell by saying,

For the good of all, with harm to none
By leaf and thunder, this spell is done!

Let the candle burn until it goes out on its own. You may keep the leaves or return them to nature.

Colors, Candles & Crystals

COLORS

The colors associated with Thursday are green and royal blue. Some magical texts also list purple. Why? Well, purple is a color associated with royalty, leadership, and wealth. Royal blue is the traditional color associated with Jupiter. Green is a popular shade with magic users, as it represents the earth and nature. Today, green in its many shades is often utilized in prosperity and healing spells.

Now, if you take a look at the many different magical books that are available today, you will see that just about everybody has their own opinion on which colors are assigned to which day of the week—which is why I listed three of them in this chapter. You should go with the color that seems right to you. Don't panic if the daily colors given here are not the ones that you have been working with. The best magics have personality and are tailor-made to suit your specific needs and tastes. Personalize your magics! Don't be afraid to try something new, or to experiment and have a little fun while working with color magic.

If you'd like to match up your outfit with Thursday's abundant and healing energies, then think of shades in blue and green. (Since we have already gone over purple in Wednesday's chapter, I will focus on our other Jupiter colors this time.) The various magical shades of blue and green each have their own correlations, and they are just waiting for you to give them a try.

A soft scarf that bleeds from blue to turquoise to green would be a nice choice. Colors that blend from one tone to another invoke a feeling of harmony and well-

being. Wear a deep navy suit for leadership and nobility, and a royal blue tie or blouse to correspond with Jupiter's energy and to get you and your hard work noticed!

How about a deep forest green T-shirt? That deep tone of green can invoke a little mystery and it represents the element of earth. Feeling adventurous? How about a bright lime-green blouse for energy and to ward off jealousy? Or how about slipping on a soft spring-green sweater? That shade of green invokes fresh starts, new beginnings, and harmonizes with the burgeoning power of the spring season. Finally, you could try wearing a vibrant St. Patrick's day green for prosperity and for fertility.

CANDLES

Candle colors for the day can be any or all of the above listed shades of blue and green. Go with the color you like the best. If you're more traditional, you may choose to stick with the primary shades of blue and green. If you tend to be a bit more creative, then refer to those colorful suggestions above, and experiment with your candle magic and see how things develop.

If you want to add a bit of aromatherapy to your Thursday candle spells, then try out these bewitching fragrances: honeysuckle-scented candles for prosperity; pine fragrances for healing and abundance; and mint to refresh your spirits and to bring money. If the only mint candles you are able to locate are white, no worries. White is an all-purpose color. Perhaps you could use a Jupiter-colored blue or green candle holder. You know that old saying—adapt, improvise, and overcome! Be a practical witch and try applying that philosophy to your own personal style of magic.

An Herbal Candle Spell for Abundance & Prosperity

Let's combine the herbal information with the color and candle information for a Thursday. You will need a few specific supplies for this spell, but the plants are common and easy to locate. You may not have to look very far, maybe not any farther than your own backyard.

Gather the following: two deep blue votive candles (you can switch these to purple); two green votive candles; four votive cups; a safe, flat surface to set up on; a lighter or matches; a sprig of honeysuckle; a few leaves of fresh mint; a small cluster of fresh pine needles; a six-by-six inch square of green or blue fabric; and a twelve-inch piece of ribbon (try a Jupiter color) to tie the fabric up into a charm bag.

Arrange the candles in their holders in a neat circle. Next, lay the foliage on the inside of the candle ring. Take your time and make this look as festive as you can, just make sure to keep the herbal ingredients well away from the flames. Then ground and center yourself, and repeat the following spell three times:

Jupiter's bright colors are in these candles four,
Money and abundance they will bring to my door.
Add some mint, pine, and honeysuckle to this witch's spell,
I call for health and prosperity and all will be well.

Now, I want you to imagine yourself surrounded by a bright blue-green halo of light. Envision that this light protects you, encourages abundance,

and invites prosperity in your life. Hold this imagery in place for a few moments.

Close the spell with this line.

For the good of all, with harm to none,
By color and herb, this spell is done!

Let the candles burn until they go out on their own. When the candles are finished, the herbs will be empowered and ready to go. Tuck the herbal ingredients into the center of the blue or green cloth and then gather up the edges. Tie the bundle closed with the ribbon. Ta-da! Instant charm bag!

Keep the prosperity charm bag with you, in your pocket or purse, for one week. If you care to re-empower the charm bag, repeat the spell on the following Thursday. Just place the bag in the center of the candle ring and you're good to go.

CRYSTALS

The stones and crystals that are associated with Jupiter and Thursday's energies of abundance and prosperity are the amethyst, the sapphire, and the turquoise.

Amethyst: Amethysts attract peace and spirituality. They are great stones to wear or carry with you to help alleviate stress. (I have a pair of amethyst-point earrings that I wear specifically for that purpose.) When I take the earrings off at night, I either set them on my windowsill and let the moonlight fall on them or I run them under water to cleanse them of any residual energy. That way, the next time I wear them, the stones are all refreshed, happy, and ready to go.

Sapphire: Also associated with Jupiter, these semiprecious stones are pricey. So, if you happen to own any sapphire jewelry, this would be one of the days to work magic with them. Magically, sapphires are protective and enchanting stones. This was the stone thought to be worn by powerful wizards and sorceresses in medieval times. Utilized in spells for prosperity and healing, these deep blue stones pack a magical wallop when worked into any positive spell. Try enchanting your sapphires with this little charm.

SAPPHIRE CHARM

Sapphires, magical stone of the deepest blue,
Aid and empower all charms and spells that I do.

Turquoise: Turquoise is easy to acquire as tumbled stone, and affordable when set in silver rings and pendants, or as beads with which to make your own jewelry. Yeah, I just adore turquoise. Turquoise is a lucky, healing, and money-drawing stone. It guards against disease and danger. (If the stone suddenly breaks, it's a warning to watch your back.) Also, turquoise promotes courage.

I have a turquoise beaded bracelet that I wear when I feel the need to reinforce my personal protection. You know, when you have to be around folks that simply drive you up the wall? No matter how hard you try to be nice to them, they just give off an uncomfortable vibe? Try wearing turquoise next time you have to be around them, it should help. Have you noticed anything about our stones for today? They are all the same colors as have been discussed in the color magic section: purple, blue, and blue-green. Don't you just love it when things fall neatly into place?

A Turquoise and Amethyst De-Stressing Spell

Stress and pressure are a nasty combination. Everybody faces stressful times now and again, even if things are going well for you at the moment. You know you worked so hard for that promotion or goal, and now that you've attained it, your workload increases and with it comes new pressures, higher expectations—usually from yourself—and stress.

Yuck! Don't allow yourself to get swept up in the pressure. Stop, ground, and center. Try taking a walk, or talking to your family and friends about what's bugging you. If you don't, you could wind up with high blood pressure and a lecture from you doctor about stress and what it can do to you physically. (Got that lecture myself, a few months ago.) And if you haven't figured it out by now . . . yes, I am a stereotypical Virgo.

What's a person to do? Well, this witch took a good look at herself and her life and dropped from her schedule whatever wasn't necessary. Next, I made my three teenagers pitch in around the house more. My husband, bless him, picked up the slack and I taught myself to eat more healthily, started taking walks, and began to meditate on a regular basis. So did a miraculous, stress-free change happen overnight? Nope, I had to work for it. What follows below is the spell I created to help me learn to cope with my stress and worries, and then to let them go.

This spell uses a turquoise or amethyst tumbled stone or piece of jewelry. This Jupiter's day charm will work whether you are programming tumbled stones to keep in your pocket or enchanting jewelry to help keep your stress under control. Hold the stones or jewelry in the palms of your hands.

Take a moment to calm yourself down and to release all of your anxiety and fear. Call on the God and Goddess to assist you. Now repeat the following spell three times:

A turquoise will bring wealth and luck, this much is true,

Good fortune and health from a stone of greenish-blue.

A purple amethyst for peace and to relieve nasty stress,

Now release all my anxiety, and lay my fears to rest.

Peace, serenity, and health are the order of the day,

Help me to relax and let go, and to keep stress at bay.

Close the spell by saying,

I release my stress and fears, they have no more power,

I close this spell by wind, flame, water, and flower.

Then tuck the crystals into your pocket or slip on the enchanted jewelry. Take time every day just for yourself and do something that relaxes you—read a silly romantic novel or rent a good comedy movie. Try working in the yard or just sitting outside for a bit. Relax in the sunshine and soak in this day's magical, healing energy.

Tarot Card Associations

The cards associated with Thursdays all happen to be from the suit of Pentacles. The tarot suit of Pentacles, or Coins, depending on your deck, is associated with the element of earth, prosperity, comfort, and health. So when deciding which cards to focus on, these three seemed like the most logical ones to me.

Ten of Pentacles symbolizes completion and a group of people, typically your friends and family. This is interpreted as a card of security, riches, and the affectionate emotional support that comes from close friends and a loving family. Add this card to any spells where emotional support and encouragement is needed (like in the de-stressing spell).

Nine of Pentacles stands for material success and emotional well-being. In some decks, the Nine of Pentacles is portrayed as a woman standing contentedly alone in a beautiful garden. The number nine indicates protection, peace, and serenity. Combining the number nine—which is three times three—with the element of earth makes for a card that symbolizes beauty, creativity, and achievement that has resulted from your earlier effort and experiences.

In other words, you have worked diligently to get to where you are standing. Relax and enjoy the benefits of your hard work and take the time to cherish these gifts. This tarot card is excellent to use in spells and charms designed for prosperity, abundance, and health, and also to protect what you have worked so hard to gain.

Ace of Pentacles signifies the undivided strength of the element that is associated with it. Since the element of earth is associated with material things, fertility, and physical well-being, this is just the tarot card to work with on a Thursday. This is card of generosity and the beauty of the earth. The Ace of Pentacles represents security, health, riches, and comfort.

It is a card to use when you feel good about yourself and your past achievements, and for when you are looking to add a bit of a financial boost in your life. Are you looking for a better job, a promotion, or are you simply hoping to catch a little overtime? Try working a spell with this card. And in the spirit of the Ace of Pentacles, remember to be generous and giving to others when your prosperity starts to roll in.

TEN OF COINS

NINE OF COINS

ACE OF COINS

·TERRA·

Earthy Prosperity Tarot Spell

If possible, work this prosperity spell outdoors. You will be calling on the element of earth and all of its fertile and abundant energies. If weather prohibits you from being outside, then set this up so your work area faces the direction north. Why? Because the northern direction is associated with the element of earth.

Gather the following: a green votive candle; a votive-cup candleholder; a half cup of garden soil (you can use potting soil); a saucer or small plate to hold the soil; the following tarot cards: Ace of Pentacles, Nine of Pentacles, and Ten of Pentacles (please note: the suits of Coins and Pentacles are the same thing); a lighter or matches; and a safe, flat work surface to set up on.

Place the green votive candle inside the cup. Snuggle the votive cup securely down into the soil. Arrange the cards next to the dish that holds the soil and candle. Take a few moments to center yourself. When you feel ready, light the candle and speak the following spell three times:

> *Element of earth I call, ground and strengthen me tonight.*
> *May the gods now bless this green spell candle that burns so bright.*
> *The suit of Pentacles and Coins calls for prosperity,*
> *They will help to bring health and abundance quickly to me.*

Close the spell by saying,

> *For the good of all, bringing harm to none,*
> *By the element of earth, this spell is done!*

Allow the candle to burn until it goes out on its own. If necessary, move the candle to a safe location so it can finish burning, such as a shower stall, inside an unlit fireplace, or in the empty kitchen sink. Never leave a burning candle unattended, especially outdoors.

Custom-Made Daily Magics

Well, let's see . . . abundance, prosperity, and good health has been our focus for this day. Now how about a little more information and ideas for working practical magic with one of our fascinating featured deities of the day?

Juno was the Queen of Heaven. As the matriarch of the gods, she guarded over women in every aspect of their lives. Juno was thought to have renewed her virginity every year. Similar to other goddess stories, Juno was a Triple Goddess—a Virgin who belonged to no one; a Mother and woman in the prime of her life, sexual and mature; and also a Crone, powerful, wise, and sometimes vengeful (as she made her husband's many mistresses' lives either fairly unhappy or short).

There are references to a early all-female triad of goddesses known as the Capitoline Triad. This triad consisted of Juventas, Juno, and Minerva. To the Greeks they would have been known as Hebe, Hera, and Hecate. Ultimately the triad became Juno, Minerva, and the male Jupiter. Jupiter, another of Thursday's gods, was the consort of Juno.

Juno, in her aspect as Juno Moneta, was the patron and protector of the Roman mint. The coins produced at her temples were blessed by Juno and imbued with her powers of abundance and prosperity. In another of her aspects as Juno Augusta, Juno was the goddess of an abundant harvest.

In addition, another of Juno's magical correspondences is the semiprecious stone malachite. Malachite is a beautiful green-banded stone that was also called the "peacock stone" in Italy. The peacock was a sacred animal of Juno's and the magical energies of malachite encourage health and prosperity. So, guess where we are going with all of this information? That's right, a spell for prosperity and abundance.

Juno's Prosperity Elemental Charm

This spell calls for some natural magic supplies. Try working with those affordable tumbled stones. As for the wheat stalks, look at the dried flowers and fillers in the arts and crafts shops. Ditto for the feather, or peruse a fly-tying store. (You can usually pick up a package of feathers for a few bucks.) As mentioned before, all of these magical supplies correspond with the goddess Juno in two of her prosperity-drawing aspects, Juno Augusta (the harvest mother) and Juno Moneta (patron of the Roman mint).

Gather the following supplies: a malachite stone to represent the earth element; a peacock feather to represent the element of air; three small stalks of dried wheat; a green candle for prosperity; a coordinating candleholder; a dollar bill or coin; matches or a lighter; and a safe, flat surface to set up on.

Arrange the candle, money, stone, wheat stalks, and feather to your liking. Hold the green candle in your hands and transfer a little of your personal power and desire for prosperity into the candle. Then place the candle in the holder. Set the holder on top of the currency. Light the candle and repeat the following spell three times:

Juno Moneta, Roman goddess of prosperity,
Lend your power to this elemental spell that I weave.
Juno Augusta, mother of the harvest, hear my plea,
These three golden stalks of wheat are a gift to you from me.
A peacock feather for air, and a malachite for earth,

Lady, bless me with success, abundance, and rebirth.

Close the spell by saying,

For the good of all, with harm to none,

In Juno's name, this spell is now done!

Allow the candle to burn until it goes out on its own. Pocket the stone and the bill or coin. Keep the money with you, tucked in your wallet or in your pocket. Tie up the feather somewhere prominent where you will see it every day, like the rearview mirror of your car, your dresser mirror, or a chest of drawers' handle. Tell Juno "thank you" every time you see the feather. Take the dried wheat and crumble the pieces apart. Sprinkle the seeds outside as an offering for Juno. Abundance and prosperity will find their way to you soon.

If you have enjoyed working this elemental spell, then take another look at the natural correspondences that were listed in this chapter. What do you suppose you could create for a little personalized magic? Flip back to the spell worksheet on page 187 and get busy crafting a spell or charm just for yourself.

Try wearing some honeysuckle-scented perfume to encourage prosperity. Bewitch someone by wearing deep royal blue or brighten up a dreary day by wearing lucky, prosperity-drawing green. Brew up a pot of mint tea to help increase your cash flow. Try adding a pinch of nutmeg or cinnamon to an unscented candle to encourage some fast cash. Bake up a loaf of wheat bread for the family and celebrate abundance and be thankful for all that you have.

Just by believing in yourself and working toward creating abundance and prosperity, you have already begun to transform your outlook on life. Put your game face on; think positively. Use your imagination, check Thursday's correspondence list, and see what you can conjure up for prosperity magic all by yourself. Call on the God and Goddess and bring some positive change, abundance, and prosperity into your life!

Friday

At-a-Glance Correspondences

planetary influence	Venus
planetary symbol	♀
deities	Eros, Aphrodite/Venus, Freya/Frigga
flowers & plants	rose, feverfew, violet, wild strawberry, apple tree
metal	copper
colors	pink, aqua
crystals & stones	rose quartz, amber, coral, emerald
tarot card associations	The Lovers, Two of Cups, The Empress
foods, herbs & spices	strawberries, raspberries

Daily Magical Applications

Friday is named after the Norse goddesses of love, Freya and Frigga. There seems to be a debate as to whom the day is actually named after, so I thought I would share a little information so you can decide for yourself.

In Latin this day is known as *Dies Veneris*, "Venus's day." In Greek it's *Hermera Aphrodites*, which translates to the "day of Aphrodite." In Old English this day is called *Frigedaeg*, or "Freya's day." This day has the Germanic title of *Frije-dagaz*, which, once again, could be Freya's day or Frigga's day.

Both Freya and Frigga were Norse goddesses of love and were the Teutonic equivalent of the Greco-Roman Venus/Aphrodite. However, Freya was one of the Vanir—the gods of fertility who supervised the land and sea—and she was the leader of the Valkyries. Frigga, Odin's wife, was the goddess of the heavens and of married love. She was one of the Aesir—the gods associated with battle, magic, and the sky. Freya and Frigga could be looked upon as different aspects of the same goddess. They both were called on to assist in childbirth, and then in the naming of the new baby. Frigga represented the faithful wife and loving mother, while Freya, who really captured the hearts and imagination of the Norse people, was the passionate mistress and lover.

Fridays classically are days for love, fertility, romance, and beauty magic, as well as working for happiness and friendship. So let's take a look at some of the mythology involved with this voluptuous, passionate, and luxurious day of the week, and see where it leads us.

Deities

EROS

Eros was the Greek god of love and desire. With a power as compelling as that of love and desire, it's really not a shocker that Eros played an important role in Greek myth and legend. Put aside your thoughts of a cute, naked baby boy playfully nailing folks with his bow and arrows. Eros was pictured as a winged god, but these would be strong and massive wings, not cute and dainty cherub wings. Eros is, instead, a handsome, sexy, and virile man. I suppose in modern terms women would refer to him as "a hottie"! No one was supposed to be immune, unaffected, or able to defend themselves against his powers of enchantment. This is a compelling and irresistible god.

According to some myths, Eros was thought to be one of first deities born into this world, along with Gaia (Mother Earth) and Tartarus (the Underworld). Eros was a popular guy with the artistic set over the centuries. He not only inspired desire in the common man but in the gods, goddesses, and heroes and heroines as well. Eros was believed to be held within the hearts of all the gods and men alike.

APHRODITE AND FREYA

When I first sat down to write this section, I could not decide who I should focus on. After all, both of these goddesses are associated with this Friday chapter's theme of love, fertility, beauty, and desire. So, since they both seemed to be clamoring for attention, I decided not to pick and choose, and to just talk about the both of them. It seemed like the smartest choice to me; remember your mythology? Freya was the

leader of the Valkyries, and anybody who snubbed Aphrodite was usually just begging for trouble.

Aphrodite was the Greek goddess of love, sexuality, and beauty. To the Romans she was known as Venus. There is more to Aphrodite than meets the eye; did you know that she was a mother *and* a grandmother? Aphrodite was mother to several children by many different partners. Her most long-standing lover was Ares, the god of war. She produced three children by him. She also had a child with Dionysus and a child with Hermes. She also hooked up with mortals from time to time, and had a child or two with her mortal lovers as well. In some mythologies she was also the mother of Eros (which is probably how the whole "cute baby" mix-up started). Eros married Psyche and they had a daughter named Volupta (Pleasure).

Aphrodite was, by all accounts, a celebrated goddess of her time. Her cult was popular throughout most of the Greek world. Interestingly enough, Aphrodite was not of Greek origin. Her followers came to Greece from Cyprus, where she was known as Kypris or the Lady of Cyprus. Aphrodite was described in her day as being both an awful and lovely goddess, at whose feet grass sprang up and grew. She is a goddess of the sea and of gardens; the rose, all blue flowers, seashells, dolphins, and pearls are just a few of her many magical correspondences.

According to Norse mythology, Freya was a goddess of fertility, love, and magic. Considered the most beautiful of the Norse goddesses, she is the patron of agriculture and childbirth. Freya enjoys music and flowers and is very fond of nature spirits, elves, and the fairies.

Freya was the consort of Odur or Od, another Norse deity who was a traveling god. While he was off rambling about, Freya mourned for him, and her tears fell into the sea and turned into golden amber. She rode in a chariot pulled by two huge gray cats, and her golden necklace Brisengamen was obtained by sleeping with four gold-working dwarves. She offered the dwarves anything they wanted if they would give her the necklace. What did the dwarves settle on? That each of them would get to spend the night with Freya, of course. Four nights later, the necklace was hers.

Brisengamen symbolized power, beauty, knowledge, and fertility—a gift from each element. Which makes me wonder: four dwarves, four elements, and four gifts or magical powers of the necklace . . .

Freya was associated with prophecy and magic. She also possessed the shamanistic ability to shapeshift. She could transform herself into a falcon with a magical cloak made of feathers. Freya was the leader of the Valkyries and claimed half of all of the slain warriors for her great hall. In plant magic, Freya is associated with the primrose, the rose, and the strawberry.

Magical Plants & Flowers

The plants associated with the planetary influence of Venus and Friday's magics of love and desire are the rose, feverfew, violet, and wild strawberry. The tree associated with today is the apple.

ROSE

Very few flowers have so many ties and connections to folklore and mythology as the rose. Today, rose petals are added to spells and flower charms to "speed things up." Just as in candle magic, the many colors of the rose may be used for various magical workings. Here is a nifty bit of floral mythology for you. Did you know that it was originally thought that all roses were white? The story goes that the goddess Aphrodite accidentally scratched herself on the thorns of a rose, and her blood then turned the petals of the flowers red.

This fabulous flower is well worth adding to your various spells and charms. Try a little "flower fascination" out and see how it works for you. Here is a brief list of the various colors of roses and their magical meanings.

red	romantic love
red and white	creativity and solidarity
orange	vitality, energy, and stamina
coral	admiration, charm
pink	friendship, beauty, and elegance

yellow	joy and happiness
ivory	romance and a steadfast, mature love
white	new beginnings and innocence
purple	power and passion
burgundy	desire and ardor

According to some plant folklore, a seven-petaled rose signified the seven days of the week. A five-petaled rose is a symbol for the Goddess, as the shape resembles a pentagram. In mythology, there are many goddesses with ties to the rose, including Freya, Diana, Flora, Juno, Selene, and the Faerie Queen Titania.

FEVERFEW
Feverfew is a great magical flowering herb. Its tiny, daisylike blossoms make terrific fillers in arrangements, and eating a few of the herb's green leaves is supposed to alleviate migraines. The feverfew plant is a protective one and may be added to charm bags or worked into herbal spells to protect you from accidents and maintain good health.

VIOLET
The violet is used in magical potpourri and charm bags to cure distress, encourage a romantic love, and to absorb negativity and manipulations. The violet is sacred to Venus/Aphrodite, as are most of the true blue flowers. The blue violet signifies hu-

mility, while a white violet stands for the truth. If you gather violets in the spring and tie them together to form a chain, or necklace, you may wear this to protect yourself from deception and from the fairies' mischievous ways. This information may come in handy, especially on Beltane Eve.

WILD STRAWBERRY

The strawberry is associated with love and good luck. The foliage and small berries of the wild strawberry may be worked into floral fascinations and charm to encourage fertility and desire. Those wild strawberry weeds that you find in the garden come in handy for natural magic. Allow them a small spot where they can grow. I have a small patch that grows under my privacy fence. I leave the dainty berries for the birds and incorporate the foliage into hand-held bouquets called tussie-mussies, or into various herbal spells and charms. In the language of flowers, the wild strawberry plant symbolizes perfection.

APPLE TREE

The apple tree is a tree of ancient magical lore and power. The apple is a sacred symbol of Aphrodite, and to many magical cultures, including the Celts, the Norse, and the Druids. The apple is used in magic for love, healing, and inspiration; it is also linked to both Freya and Aphrodite. Apple blossoms may be added to spells designed to encourage romance, or they may be scattered around your altar or circle to celebrate Friday and love and fertility.

Having trouble choosing between two lovers? An old apple charm tells you to take two apple seeds from an apple that you have just eaten. Then name the seeds, one for each lover, and stick one seed to each facial cheek. Here is a modern version of the apple seed charm.

∂

APPLE SEED CHARM

Apple seed, apple seed, I place you here on my cheek.
Show me the love that is true, will be faithful and sweet.

Whichever seed stays on your face longer denotes your true love and a faithful partner.

There are dozens of plant and flower associations for love, Venus, and Fridays. However, I like to keep things practical and list easy-to-find flowers, trees, and herbs. So what do we do now? Let's take all of this herbal information and whip up a little Friday romance-inducing fertility spell.

The Apples/Strawberries & Roses Fertility Spell

Thinking about increasing your family or perhaps starting one? Call on the goddesses Aphrodite or Freya for a little assistance. These ladies can help you achieve your goal of a successful pregnancy and a safe delivery.

For this spell you will need two ripe apples, one for you to snack on and the other for your partner. If you do not care for apples, then try strawberries. Strawberries are sacred to Freya, and let's face it—ripe, fresh, and deeply red strawberries are a sexy food. (If you choose to go with strawberries then adjust the spell's opening line accordingly.) You will also need a fresh red rose in a vase to symbolize your love for each other. If you choose, you may add a few rosy-pink candles to this spell for some atmosphere. You know what sets a romantic mood for the two of you, so follow your instincts. Try working this fertility spell during a waxing moon. You may say this charm together, silently or aloud.

> *Symbols of the Goddess, apples/berries and a rose of red,*
> *We call for fertility to follow us to bed.*
> *Love and pleasure are her rituals, this is true,*
> *Goddess bless us with a child, make us parents soon.*

Don't forget while you are working toward this goal to be romantic, to have fun, relax, and let nature take its course.

Colors, Candles & Crystals

COLORS

The colors associated with Friday and the planetary influence of Venus are pink and aqua green. The color pink is often used to promote friendship and affection, and it can also be worked into children's magic.

Green in all of its shades promotes health and fertility. Aqua green works into Friday's magic nicely, as the elemental association for Friday is water—which makes sense as Venus/Aphrodite rose from the sea and this hue of sea green is sacred to her.

If you would enjoy incorporating a little color magic into your wardrobe, try pinks in shades from pale to rosy mauves—a silky shirt in a deep carmine pink, a soft sweater in pastel pink, or what about a floaty, flirty dress in bright pink? You could coordinate your ensemble by wearing shades of mauve and rose for cosmetics.

If you aren't comfortable wearing pink, try strawberry red, or look at various sea-green colors. Use your imagination.

CANDLES

Candle colors for this romantic day once again will be shades of pink and aqua green. If you'd like to experiment with a little magical candle aromatherapy, then look to floral and rose-scented candles. These scents will encourage love and romance and will promote a relaxed atmosphere. Also, see if you can find any pale-green, apple-scented candles. The scent of apples is a good one to promote love and healing. It also dispels bad vibes and negativity. The apple has ties to both of our featured goddesses for the day. If you are petitioning one of these ladies, this should help to gain their attention and their help.

Drawing Love and Romance Spell

This candle spell is designed to draw a little romance and love into your life. Like always, remember not to target anyone specific here. We want to pull a little romantic fun and excitement into your life, not take away another's free will.

Gather the following supplies: a pink floral-scented votive; a pale green apple-scented votive; two votive cups; a rose and a bud vase or fresh, loose rose petals (match the color of the flower to your magical intention: see page 139); lighter or matches; and a safe, flat work area to set up on.

Arrange the candles and the flower or flower petals in a way that pleases you. Try scattering the petals around the outside of the votive cups in a circle or setting the flower in a bud vase off to the side. Light the candles and repeat the following spell three times:

Roses and candles, symbols of desire and love,

Aphrodite hear my call, send your help from above.

Send to me a lover who is fun, faithful, and true,

Guide my magic, and assist me in all that I do.

Close the spell by saying,

For the good of all, with harm to none,

By candle and rose, this spell is done!

Let the candles burn until they go out on their own. Keep the rose in the vase until it begins to fade, then crumble the petals apart and allow them to air dry. If you used loose petals, allow those to dry out as well. After the petals have dried you may add them to a charm bag and keep it with you to encourage loving vibrations, or return them to nature as an offering to the Goddess.

Note: If you decide to reword this spell to suit your own needs, then please be very specific. If you go overboard on the "love me" theme and work for an existing spouse or lover to become more passionate or devoted to you, you could suddenly find yourself with an obsessive partner who never leaves your side. They may become jealous or never allow you any privacy. And no, I am not trying to spook you. Just think of this a friendly reminder and consider yourself warned, and be very careful what you spell-cast for—especially when it comes to love.

CRYSTALS

The crystals and stones linked to Friday and the planetary influence of Venus are the ones that draw love, healing, and power: the emerald and coral. We also have a few other rather obvious crystals to consider. The rose quartz, to encourage loving vibra- tions and "warm fuzzies," and the amber, which is Freya's special stone. Amber is a healing stone that promotes beauty and strength, and is actually a fossilized resin from coniferous trees. Amber is typically warm to the touch and is a powerful stone uti- lized for almost every magical purpose. From love and fertility magic to prosperity to increasing personal power and protection, amber's got it all covered.

Now, while these last two stones do not traditionally fall under the planetary in- fluence of Venus, they certainly harmonize with our theme of the day. Both of these stones are fairly easy to obtain and are a great link to the featured Friday goddesses.

Aphrodite's Crystal Beauty Ritual

This ritual calls for an inner beauty—the sort of loveliness that just shines right through, sort of a magical sparkle. With this thought in mind, Aphrodite can help you learn to love yourself just as you are, curvy and voluptuous or athletic and angular. Take a look at those old statues and paintings of the goddesses sometime. Notice anything different? They have curves! Real people have curves—learn to embrace yours and don't worry so much about your clothing size. Beautiful, bewitching, and enchanting women (and men for that matter) come in all different shapes, colors, and sizes. The Aphrodite image that is so popular depicts a woman with rounded thighs and a curved tummy, and she is a knockout. So take a hint from Aphrodite and be voluptuous, sexy, and proud of who you are!

Start off this Friday night ritual by taking a relaxing tub bath. Toss a few teaspoons of sea salt into your water for its cleansing purposes. If you wish, you may light a few floral-scented candles and sprinkle a few rose petals on the water. After you've indulged in a nice long soak, step out of the tub and dry off. Slip on a robe or comfortable outfit. Gather together a few supplies and settle down in your favorite magical space.

The supplies to gather include: a rose quartz tumbled stone; coral beads or a stone (an inexpensive coral beaded bracelet would work out great); a pink or aqua green candle; a few seashells for Aphrodite, who was a sea-born goddess; a white flower in a vase, and a rose or other white garden flower (use whatever is handy).

Arrange the components of this spell however you would like. Improvise, personalize, and set this up how you prefer. Light the candles and then repeat the following spell three times:

Seashells, a rosy quartz, and coral beads,

Aphrodite, your help I do now seek.

Cause my eyes to sparkle, bring a glow to my skin,

As I deepen the beauty that comes from within.

Close the ritual with this line,

By all the powers of land and sea,

As I will it, then so shall it be.

When you are finished with your ritual, allow the candles to burn out in a safe place. Keep the stones or loose beads with you for one week. If you used a piece of jewelry, then wear the jewelry for the same amount of time.

Have fun with this "inner beauty" ritual and may you walk through life as Aphrodite herself did, proudly and with an inner beauty.

Tarot Card Associations

The tarot cards related to Friday and the qualities of love, fertility, beauty, and relationships are typically from the suit of Cups, which in some decks may be called Cauldrons. No matter what the title, this water-associated suit symbolizes love, fertility, and emotions. All of the following tarot cards link up with Friday's theme quite nicely:

> ***The Lovers*** is one card that even folks who only have a passing acquaintance with a tarot deck know about. The symbolism is fairly obvious. The Lovers card symbolizes an important emotional commitment may be in the future, like a wedding. But what most folks don't realize is that while this card can signify a romantic relationship, it also represents choice.
>
> This means that when this card shows up in a reading, there is a choice to be made. It may be between two individuals or it could be between two opportunities. This card would be a good prop to add to the Apple Seed Charm that was listed earlier in this chapter. The Lovers is a symbol of options, decisions, and commitments.
>
> ***Two of Cups*** is a card that mainly deals with emotions and relationships. It may represent an engagement, an affair, or a marriage. This card may also signify a close friendship, a mother and child, or a good business partnership. This card shows that there is someone special in your life,

someone you trust and to whom you turn when the chips are down. This card is a wonderful tool to add to any spells designed to promote friendship, partnership, love, and marriage.

The Empress: This card can represent the Mother aspect of the Goddess. It usually depicts a woman in a ripe field of grain or in a natural and fertile environment, such as in a forest, next to a stream. Typically the

woman is surrounded by grains, flowers, and fruits; often she is shown as pregnant to denote her fertility. She has a "Mother Nature" look about her and symbolizes a happy home, comfort, happy marriage, love, sex, childbirth, and motherhood.

Try adding the Empress card to the fertility spell that was listed earlier in this chapter. If you are already pregnant, set up this card next to a white candle and focus on the symbolism. Meditate on the idea of the Mother aspect of the Goddess and ask her to protect you and your unborn child throughout the pregnancy. If you would like to work a spell to safeguard your pregnancy and to ensure a safe delivery, try this tarot spell.

A Tarot Spell for Pregnancy & Childbirth

For this spell you will need the following supplies: a green or white candle and matching holder, or a plain seven-day candle; the tarot cards the Empress and the Two of Cups; grains (dried barley or stalks of wheat, or a bit of whole wheat flour); a cauldron, cup, or small bowl to hold the grains; an item of sympathy for the baby, like a baby bootie or an ultrasound photo; a pink and baby blue satin ribbon to tie around the candle holder; an item of sympathy for the mother, such as a small lock of her hair, a photo of her or the two of you taken while she's pregnant; and a few fresh flowers in a vase (use whatever is in season, in the garden, or affordable).

If your due date is fast approaching, you might want to set up this spell where you can see it every day. Try the top of your dresser or on a shelf in the living room. If you prefer, try one of those large, seven-day types of candles. (You know, the kind that comes in a tall glass jar.) That way you can light and relight the candle as the mood suits you. If you are working this spell for your partner, make sure to get their permission and try working the spell together, as a couple about to become a family.

Set up this spell in an arrangement that pleases you. Place the grains or flour inside of the cauldron to keep the area tidy. Try propping up the tarot cards and photo against the candle, cup, or cauldron. During the pregnancy, I would repeat the spell once a month. As you get into the last week of the pregnancy, I would repeat it every day. (The seven-day candle will come in handy for that.) If you are working this together as a couple, then adjust the words accordingly.

Great Mother I call, protect and watch over me today,
Bless this child that I carry, as it grows stronger each day.
Tokens of fertility are the grains and the flowers,
Candles and cards are symbols of a new mother's power.
Guard us both during the labor and delivery,
Help me to be strong, and to have a healthy baby.

Friday

Close the spell with this line,

> *By the Mother Goddess, the moon and sun,*
> *By the power of love, this spell is done.*

Allow the candle to burn for as long as you wish, just be sure to keep an eye on it. Replace the grains and flowers with fresher ones as needed. Good luck to your family, and best wishes for a safe delivery and a happy, healthy baby!

Custom-Made Daily Magics

Here are a couple of spells for you to experiment with. These spells fit right in with our chapter's theme of love and romance. They feature two of our deities for Friday, Eros and Freya. The first spell works with the Greek god of passion, Eros. This spell is designed to bring a little more drive and passion into your life, and is easy and simple, with few supplies, so you will be able to set it up and perform it quickly. It will help you get inspired, enthusiastic, and fired up to face your challenges and to embrace life.

Eros's "Passion for Life" Spell

Gather the following supplies: a white feather (symbol for eros and his mighty wings); a rosy pink candle; and a coordinating candleholder.

Carve a simple figure of a bow and arrow on the side of the candle. Place the feather off to the side, away from the heat of the candle flame. Picture the winged god Eros in your mind and meditate on this image for a moment. Now, ask Eros in your own words to inspire you with passion and enthusiasm. Then repeat the following spell three times:

Eros, winged Greek god of passion and delight,

Aid me in my quest for inspiration tonight.

Passion is more than sexual, it conveys ambition too,

Help me face my challenges, and succeed in all that I do.

Allow the candle to burn out in a safe place. Close the spell by saying,

For the good of all, with harm to none,
By flame and feather, this spell is done.

Freya's Jewelry Spell

Last but not least, here is a quick spell to work with the energies of the Norse goddess Freya. Freya was the mistress of cats and a supreme goddess of magic, sexuality, and enchantment. The idea behind this Friday-Freya's night spell is to empower and to protect your magical jewelry.

Most witches wear special jewelry and it's easy to forget to recharge those magical pieces from time to time. Since Freya went above and beyond to obtain her sacred necklace Brisengamen, I think she'll work out beautifully for this next spell. (And no, you don't have to sleep with any goldsmithing dwarves to get it to work, either.) Look over the supply list carefully. If you are allergic to cats, then use a photo of one to focus on in the spell. Feel free to arrange this however you'd like. In case you haven't noticed, I have been harping on that individualizing and personalizing theme for quite a while now—so have fun, harm none, and be imaginative.

Gather the following: the jewelry to be enchanted; an amber tumbling stone; a pale green candle for Friday; a gold candle for Freya; two coordinating candleholders; and a photo of a cat or a few strands of loose cat hair. (Let's be absolutely clear on this ingredient. Do not pull hair from a live cat. If you gently pet any cat, a few stray hairs are bound to shed off of their coat. You'll only need a few, and those loose hairs will work out fine. If you work with shed hair, then place the cat hair under the candles and within the candleholders.)

Light the candles, ground, and center. Then pass the jewelry between the two candle flames. Be careful not to burn your fingers. Repeat the following spell for each piece of jewelry:

Freya, goddess of magic, enchant this jewelry of mine,
May I work with these wisely, any place and at all times.

You may save the candles to reuse at a later time, if you wish. I would recommend recharging your magical pieces once a month, during a waxing moon. Another incredible boost to this spell would be to work it on Friday the thirteenth. Since thirteen was a sacred number to Freya and Fridays are named after her, you can't get much better than that.

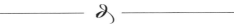

Fridays are days of loving enchantments and passionate emotions. Take a good look at this chapter, peruse that spell worksheet on page 187, and adapt or create a few spells of your own. See how many ways you could add a little loving enchantment into your life and the lives of your loved ones.

Try sharing some red berries with your partner some enchanted evening. Wear a Venus color and call on the Goddess for a little inner sparkle. Burn some floral incense, light up some rosy candles, and set a romantic mood. Advancing your magical skills takes drive, ambition, and passion. Work with Eros and discover just how much enthusiasm, inspiration, and drive he can bring into your days.

The imagination is a place where dreams flourish and ideas come to fruition. Call on these fertile and romantic powers and create your own unique spells and charms. Just think of all the magical information that you can now add to your repertoire. Lastly, remember this: when you combine imagination and a loving heart with magic, you'll succeed every time.

Saturday

How pleasant is Saturday night,
when I've tried all week to be good.

Nancy Sproat (1766–1827)

planetary influence	Saturn
planetary symbol	♄
deities	Saturn, Hecate
flowers & plants	pansy, morning glory, mullein, cypress tree
metal	lead
colors	black, deep purple
crystals & stones	obsidian/Apache tear, hematite, jet
tarot card associations	Temperance, Knight of Swords, Two of Swords
foods, herbs & spices	pomegranate, beets, thyme

Daily Magical Applications

Saturday, our final featured day of the week, gets its name from the Latin *Dies Saturni,* or "Saturn's day." In Old English, it was *Saeturnesdaeg.* The Middle English version was *Saterday.* Saturn, a Roman god of agriculture, was believed to have ruled the Earth during an age of contentment and virtue. Saturn was a god who symbolized the passage of time and karma. He was not a harsh, judgmental god, either; he was a sower and a harvester.

Saturdays are traditionally days to work on protection, remove obstacles, bind troublesome or dangerous individuals, and banish negativity. Saturdays are like a magical "let's clean house" day. Any magical messes left lying around that need to be addressed, or any problems that need to be cleared up, are best dealt with on the day devoted to Saturn.

Deities

SATURN

An ancient Roman god also known as Father Time, Saturn was called the Ruler of the Golden Age and the Father of the Gods. Saturn was considered the "Great Lesson Giver," as he required people to learn their lessons through karma. Saturn was also a god of agriculture and fertility, and was married to a fertility goddess named Ops.

There is a Roman festival named after him called the Saturnalia. This seven-day, rowdy, midwinter festival was a time of gift-giving, feasts, and partying. The wine flowed freely and the slaves were given the holiday off. Schools closed and the military was given leave. What was Saturnalia like? It was probably very similar to Mardi Gras today.

Saturn was described as a man with a half-bared chest, holding a sickle and a few ears of corn. This image of Saturn eventually evolved into our Father Time, a popular image at New Year's Eve. The sickle became the scythe and the hourglass symbolized the passing of time and Saturn's control over it. Saturn is not a frightening god—he is a teacher, a spiritual influence that grants tranquility and calmness in your later years. Saturn is the guardian of time.

HECATE

Hecate was the daughter of Perses and one of the original Titans. Even after Zeus defeated the Titans, he kept Hecate in power to assist the mortals. Zeus honored Hecate greatly by granting her a share of power over the earth, the sky, and the sea.

Mortals who were favored by Hecate received great blessings, as she could increase the size of their herds or help the fishermen who prayed to her haul in huge catches of fish.

Originally considered a generous and compassionate ancient fertility goddess, in later myths Hecate became associated with a darker and more frightening magic. She developed into the patron of sorcerers and became associated with the underworld, dark mysteries, crossroads, and graveyards. Hecate became known as the Queen of the Witches and the Guardian of the Crossroads.

Some of the more well-known associations for Hecate are keys, black dogs, torches, and the three-way crossroads. Hecate was frequently pictured as triple-faced deity. There are a few variations on her name as well—Hecate Trivia or Hekate, often looked on as the Crone aspect of another trio of Greco-Roman goddesses, these being Persephone the Maiden, Demeter the Mother, and Hecate the Crone.

Hecate was thought to be all-seeing and wise. When Demeter searched everywhere for her daughter Persephone, who had been snatched by Hades into the underworld to be his bride, it was Hecate who finally told Demeter where she was. Today Hecate is a powerful and protective deity for witches. If you feel the need to defend yourself, your property, or your family, Hecate is the one to call on. Her sacred plants include mints, cyclamen, and the willow tree.

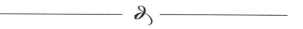

Magical Plants & Flowers

The flowers associated with the planetary influence of Saturn are the pansy, morning glory, and mullein. One of the trees associated with Saturday is the cypress.

PANSY

The pansy, or viola, is a common garden flower with a lot of magical *oomph* behind it. Available in a myriad of colors, it is a happy, unassuming, protective flower that many magical practitioners grow in their gardens but never put to work. Besides their qualities of healing a broken heart, they also speak of happy thoughts. The pansy has many folk names, including heartsease, Johnny jump-up, and love-in-idleness.

If you choose to work protective charms with the pansy, then look for the dark purple and black ones. The deeper the color of the pansy, the more protective energy it will produce. There are black pansies available for you to work into your flower fascinations as well—look for the variety called "Black Magic." Plant some deep, jewel-toned pansies in a container or add them to your semi-shady borders for a little mystery and drama in the garden. ***Note:*** Pansies will perform their best in the spring and fall months. They dislike hot weather.

MORNING GLORY

The morning glory is a favorite cottage-style plant of mine. These annual climbing vines can grow over fifteen feet in height in just one season. The deep-blue blooms open in September and the vines, foliage, and flowers may be worked into protec-

tion spells and bindings. If you choose to work with morning glory vines for a binding, snip off a small section of the vine and wrap it around your item of sympathy. If this is a troublesome person then you could wrap the vine around a photo, or a sample of their handwriting. Or take an old, clean, glass jar and put the item of sympathy inside, then stuff the jar full of morning glory leaves and vines. Bury or dispose of the jar off of your property.

MULLEIN

Mullein is a wildflower that grows in dry, rocky, disturbed ground. Folk names for mullein include "graveyard dirt" and "hag's tapers." The latter name started because in olden times, the flower stalks were soaked in tallow and then set aflame to be used as long-lasting torches. The mullein is a biennial that produces large stalks of yellow flowers up to eight feet in height. The flower stalks bloom from the bottom up and the large leaves are soft and fuzzy. (Sort of a gigantic version of lamb's ears.) Mullein leaves are thought to keep away all negative intentions and evil. Carrying a leaf was supposed to protect its bearer from attack and from harm. Dried and crushed, mullein leaves may be used as a substitute for real graveyard dirt, should you ever find yourself in need of some.

CYPRESS TREE

The cypress tree, a symbol for immortality and eternity, has the startling folk name of "the tree of death." This may be because of its link to Hecate and darker magics, or it may simply be due to the fact that it is a tree often found in European graveyards and was once a popular wood with the Egyptians for building coffins. Some varieties of this grand evergreen may grow over 100 feet in height. The cypress has grayish-brown bark and small green foliage (needles). There is also a native cypress to the Southwestern United States called the Arizona cypress. This tree has more of a silvery-blue color to its foliage. It is utilized to help stop erosion and treasured for its ability to adapt to harsh climates.

Cypress oil is a popular ingredient in colognes and soaps, as its scent is bracing and clean. Carrying a piece of cypress wood was thought to bring you a long life, and when the tree was planted near the home it bestowed blessings and protection on the habitants of the house. Cypress may be used to construct a wand for healing purposes, or to be used when working with the goddess Hecate.

Why not combine some of the plant folklore and magical herbal information from this chapter into a protective spell with ingredients that you can probably find in your own gardens?

Garden Witch Protection Spell

This spell is designed to stop bad feelings and harsh words between two friends. It's tough when a person that you considered your friend turns against you for whatever reason. Perhaps you quarreled or you have simply grown apart. In these situations, however, now that the feud is on, your defenses are low. Emotions can be raw and feelings may be hurt very easily on both sides. Why? Probably because you know each other well enough to know exactly which buttons to push. If you feel that you've hit your limit on what you can handle, then try this protection spell designed to end the fight and let the both of you heal and move forward in a positive way.

Gather the following: a single stem of blooming snapdragons (if you recall from Tuesday's chapter, snapdragons break manipulative energies and are very protective magical flowers); dark purple pansies—a bloom or two will suffice; a black satin ribbon; and a six-by-six inch square of dark purple or black fabric.

Take a few of the snapdragon blooms and a pansy flower and place them in the center of the cloth square. Repeat the spell below three times and on the final saying, gather up the sides of the bag and tie it closed with the black ribbon. Knot the bag three times.

Snapdragons, snap back at negativity,
End the quarrel between my friend and me.
Pansies are a sure cure for the brokenhearted,
Let us both move on and our relief get started!

Close the spell by saying,

> *For the good of all, with harm to none,*
> *By Saturn's energies, this spell is done.*

You may keep the charm bag on your person for as long as you need to. Allow yourself some time to mend. It won't be instantaneous, but you can reinforce this spell every Saturday as needed. When you feel that you don't need the charm bag anymore, open it up and give the floral components back to nature. Dispose of the ribbon and the fabric in a trash can somewhere away from where you live or work.

Colors, Candles & Crystals

COLORS

The colors linked with Saturn and Saturday's protective magics are black and dark purple. Yes, I agree that purple has shown up all over the daily color correspondences. Perhaps it's because it is a very popular color with magic users. There is just something mystical about it. However, for today's spells and color magic, we need the deepest, darkest purple that you can find.

Black is the classic witch's color. This midnight hue is a traditional color to work with and to wear on a Saturday, or anytime you want to appear in control and confident. Whether you go trendy, dramatic, and gothic, or more subdued, such as wearing a classic tailored black jacket and slacks, black is a seductive, attention-getting color for clothes.

Now, typically magic users adore colors, all colors, but we tend to save our all-black ensembles for special occasions. Honestly, doesn't everybody? No matter your religious preference, almost every woman owns a "little black dress"—something she saves for when she really wants to turn a few heads or make a confident statement.

Black is also the traditional candle color for protection magic. There is something extra intriguing and witchy about black candles. Sometimes these may be hard to locate throughout the year. Your best bet is to watch for black candles during the fall months (especially around Halloween) and stock up on them.

If you check out a few specialty or trendy candle shops at the mall, you will be able to find black jar candles and votives. It always makes me smile to see a classy jar candle labeled something like "Midsummer's Magic" or "Midnight Spice." Typically these are patchouli scented, and that is perfect to use in candle magic, as patchouli is associated with Saturn and protection. Work with either of these dramatic and dark-featured colors for Saturday candle spells designed to protect, neutralize gossip, and deflect harm.

A Black Candle Spell to Deflect Negativity

Have you had one ghastly week at work? Is bad luck plaguing you, or does everything seem to be going wrong? Maybe you simply feel that you are surrounded by everyone else's psychic garbage. Before you start to panic, stop and consider your options. Here is a candle spell to break up those bad vibes and to deflect the negativity that seems to be surrounding you.

All this time you've been waiting for the perfect excuse to get all vamped up and to break out the black candles. This dramatic spell is a favorite of my teenage daughter, as she loves any excuse to be theatrical and as witchy as possible. For this spell you'll need to go all out: black clothes, dark makeup (if you wish), and several black candles. Play your favorite magical music—Native American drums, haunting Celtic tunes, or a dreamy synthesizer piece—whatever you find particularly inspiring or magical.

When should you work this spell? Set it up late Friday night and, as the clock strikes midnight, signaling the start of a new Saturday, light the altar candles and begin the spell.

Gather the following: a black piece of cloth or scarf to drape over your work area; three black candles, two votives and one taper (use the votives as altar candles for illumination, and the taper candle to represent the negativity you are fighting); three coordinating candleholders; matches or a lighter; and a brown paper lunch bag.

Note: One of these candles must be a taper, as you need to be able to easily snap the candle in half during this spell. This is a quick spell, but effective. Ground and center yourself before you begin this spell, and remove all hatred from your heart. Put yourself into a determined and practical state of mind, and then get to work. Begin speaking the charm as the clock strikes twelve.

As the clock strikes midnight, this candle spell now takes place,
Fear and dread be gone, I banish you from time and space!

Light the black taper. Take a few moments and visualize all of the negativity and problems that you need safely removed from your life.

This black candle represents all the negativity
With magic, I break the bad luck that is surrounding me.

Pinch out the candle and then snap the taper in half.

By the powers of the moon, the stars, and the sun,
As I will, so mote it be, and let it harm none.

Place the broken taper candle into the lunch bag. Fold the bag closed and drip a bit of the votive candle wax on it to seal the spell. You may allow the votive illuminator candles to burn until they go out on their own, or save them and reuse them for another Saturday spell.

Take the paper bag holding the candle and remove it from your property. This represents the negativity that has been surrounding you, so let's get rid of it. Take a walk or a drive and toss it into a public garbage can, somewhere away from your house and away from where you work. Once it's been disposed of, turn your back and don't look back. Put all of this garbage behind you.

CRYSTALS

The crystals and stones that are connected to Saturday and the energies of Saturn are useful for grounding, centering, protection, and for absorbing negativity. Look for obsidian or Apache tear, hematite, jet, and smoky quartz. (Even though a quartz crystal is technically not associated with Saturn, the smoky quartz is still a great protective stone for grounding and repelling negative emotions.)

Obsidian is a naturally occurring glass. It's lava that cooled so quickly that the minerals inside of it did not have time to form. Sometimes this black, translucent stone is called Apache tear and you may also find obsidian with white patterns in it—this variety is called "snowflake obsidian." No matter what variety you discover, this is a great stone to help you ground and center. An excellent choice to add to any Saturday spell, obsidian is a popular stone to utilize in protective spells and

magics designed to fight negativity and break bad luck. Check out a few stores that carry inexpensive tumbled stones and pick up a few to have on hand.

Hematite is a solid and heavy-feeling silvery-black colored stone. This stone is popular for its grounding and calming properties. Hematite is a stabilizer and you may often find rings carved out of it. Hematite was also used in healing rituals, so if you wanted to, this would be a great stone to add to any spells designed to help feuding friends heal and move on.

Jet has the folk name of witches' amber or black amber, probably due to the fact that many High Priestesses wear beads of amber and jet to denote their rank. According to *Cunningham's Encyclopedia of Crystal, Gem & Metal Magic*, jet becomes electronically charged when it is rubbed. Jet is a sympathetic stone and will absorb pessimistic or negative energies. It can be placed in a heavily trafficked room in your home to absorb bad vibes or to absorb anger. If jet is placed in the bedroom, it promotes a good night's sleep and guards against nightmares. Try placing jet around a candle and then focus your intentions on creating a happy and argument-free zone in your home. Set the candle and the stones somewhere in the most-used room in the house and silently let them do their work.

If you are the sort of person who really wants or needs a fast spell that is no muss, no fuss, then try this all-purpose charm to go along with any crystal and candle magic that you perform.

By the strength of the earth and the power of fire,
May these crystals now bring the outcome I desire.

A Crystal Protection Spell

Try this crystal and stone spell for protection and a little help in boosting your personal shields. Sometimes we all need to boost our auras or energy shields. Whether you are recovering from being sick or just feeling vulnerable at the moment, this spell ought to do the trick.

Gather the following: four of this chapter's featured protective stones and crystals; any style white candle; a coordinating candleholder; a photo of yourself; a lighter or matches; and a safe, flat surface to set up on.

First things first. Take a shower or a bath and imagine that all of the negativity you've been carrying around is being washed away by the age-old cure of running water. Step out of the shower, dry off, and slip on a favorite comfy outfit or robe. Find a good spot on which to set up this spell—try a shelf or a fireplace mantle. Maybe you'll want to use your nightstand. Just

make sure you are setting the candle in a safe place, away from small children or pets.

Situate the photo off to the side of the candle and holder. Surround the photo with the four protective stones. Visualize yourself surrounded by a dazzling white light and a strong protective energy. Repeat the following spell three times.

Crystals and stones of protection and power,

Lend your strength to me in this magic hour.

Safety and security this quick spell now yields,

As I increase my energy and boost my shields.

Close the spell by saying,

For the good of all, with harm to none,

By flame and crystal, this spell is done!

You should know the drill by now—allow the candle to burn out. Pocket the stones and keep them with you for a week.

Tarot Card Associations

The tarot cards that correspond with Saturday's protective and troubleshooting energy are Temperance, the Knight of Swords, and the Two of Swords. The suit of Swords often represents conflict, power, decisions, and judgment. The Major Arcana card featured in this final chapter is Temperance. This card symbolizes moderation and patience, a way of maintaining a sort of inner balance. These are the qualities we will want to tap into for our Saturday spellwork.

Temperance is a Major Arcana card that typically shows a female winged figure pouring liquid from one cup into another. While some folks assume that this is an angel, this winged figure has probable pagan origins. (Think of Isis and her sister, Nepthys—both of these goddesses had wings.) The Temperance card may be used in spells designed to help you find the "right balance." This symbolism can assist you in finding a way to harmoniously blend all of the aspects of your life. When the Temperance card appears in a tarot reading, it means that the person has a mature and balanced personality, and that they can handle difficult situations with diplomacy and competence. This is the sort of tone or imagery that we want to invoke for Saturday spells.

The Knight of Swords can be summed up in two words: "No fear." The Knight of Swords symbolizes a person who is fearless. They ride into situations and handle even the most difficult things in a spirited and competent fashion. This card in a reading symbolizes a direct, honest,

and open person. This is the tarot card to work with when dealing with a conflict or argument with another person. This type of energy comes in handy when you are breaking negativity or attempting to deal fairly with a difficult person.

Two of Swords: Many of the cards in the suit of Swords represent struggle or conflict. However, the Two of Swords stands for balance and restored peace. This card speaks of two equal forces that have maintained a balance. Neither is better than the other; they are both just as strong, or as right. In magic this card invokes a truce and a cautious peace. Work with this card when you are trying to create a peaceful resolution to a problem and when justice is the issue. This card will help ensure that the magic turns out fairly for everyone involved. Now, with that idea in mind, here is a tarot spell to try when you need to call for justice and harmony.

Tarot Spell for Justice and Peace

Here is our final tarot spell, and it's a doozy. Remember to work your spells honestly and ethically, especially when you call for justice. Justice is a neutral force. It doesn't take sides or play favorites. The scales will be weighed for you as well. So be honest and fair in both your magical and mundane dealings.

Gather the following: the tarot cards Temperance, Two of Swords, and the Knight of Swords; one black candle; one white candle; one gray candle; three candleholders; mullein flowers or leaves (to banish negativity); and matches or a lighter. Have a safe, flat surface to set up the spell on.

Arrange the herb and cards to your liking between the white and black candles. Set the gray candle, symbolizing neutrality, in its holder directly behind the cards. The white and black candles symbolize balance and represent the two opposing forces that are at work.

If you choose, you can personalize this spell by adding an item of sympathy. If this is a legal matter, perhaps you could add a letter from your attor-

ney. If it's personal, you could add an item that was given to you as a gift by the other party. Be creative! Take a few moments to ground and center. Calm yourself and hold the idea in your mind for the fairest and best possible outcome. Repeat the following spell three times.

The Knight of Swords, a symbol for courage under fire,
Hear my call for protection, it's justice I desire!
The Two of Swords settles conflicts and does invoke peace so fair,
Add Temperance for balance, and a bit of personal flair.
Lord and Lady, hear my cry, defend and watch over me,
Help me settle this fairly; as I will, so mote it be.

Close the spell by saying,

In no way will this tarot spell reverse,
Or place upon me or mine any curse.

Allow the candles to burn until they go out on their own. Straighten your work area when finished and tuck the Temperance card into your wallet, purse, or day planner. Carry it with you until the following Saturday, then return it to your tarot deck.

Custom-Made Daily Magics

Protection, removing negativity, justice, and balance have been the theme of this final chapter. Here is a magical topic that gets a lot of attention: bindings. What about bindings? Can you perform one and not cross the ethical line? Absolutely. I have heard of some witches who paint a mental white X over a criminal's face when they see them on television or read about them in the paper. If this is someone that you personally know, who is causing you or your family harm, it is possible to use a photograph of the destructive person. Simply wrap white ribbon around their photo to symbolize you binding them up. Poppets may be employed as well. But be careful. Sometimes, when you bind a person, you are actually binding their energy more closely to yourself.

So what is your best course of action? To remove all emotion from your self and the spell when you perform the binding. Just as I stated before, justice—like magic—is a neutral force. For lack of a better term, be businesslike. Wild swings of emotion only make for an uncontrollable magical energy. Therefore, your best bet is to be neutral. If there was ever a time to be calm and in control, this is it.

Bindings are best performed on a Saturday. A binding is the act of psychically restraining a harmful person or criminal so that their actions cannot harm anyone else. The goddess to call on is Hecate, a mighty magical force. Consider your words and actions carefully when you call on her. How you choose to work a binding is up to you. At this point, I strongly suggest that you take a moment and draft out your binding spell on paper. Refer to the worksheet on page 187, it will help you. Go

carefully and remember to harm none. Don't be taken aback if you begin to notice barking or howling dogs. They sense when Hecate is near.

Yes, we have gotten very serious all of a sudden. That's because a binding is a serious matter. Surprised? Don't be. Just because I tend to look at things from a humorous perspective doesn't mean I am not serious when the situation calls for it.

This invocation includes some of the correspondences for Hecate. If you choose, you can add these to your spellwork. A general invocation for Hecate follows.

INVOCATION TO HECATE

Cauldrons, three keys, and black dogs that bay at the moon,
Grant me wisdom and strength, pray hear this witch's tune.
Goddess of the Crossroads, Hecate, I call on you,
Come lend your magic to mine; my need is strong and true.

Note: Remember to thank Hecate for her time and attention when you are finished with your magic.

Saturdays are the particular day of the week for protection and for dealing with more serious magical matters. Go back over the "at a glance" list and see what components you can add to your spells for today for a little more *oomph*.

ව

And Saturday Makes Seven

Well, we have just about wrapped things up with this chapter and this little book of correspondences. Before we part, here are a few more quick and practical ideas for magic on a Saturday. Feel the need for a psychic cleansing in the house? Light up some patchouli-scented incense and wave the smoke around your house or apartment. It will help to break up any lingering negativity or bad feelings. Crumble up a few dried mullein leaves and create a circle around your home, or scatter it across the thresholds, to keep prowlers away.

Burn a few black candles to repel manipulative intentions or unwanted advances. Add a few protective herbs to your dinner such as thyme or basil. Try growing a cyclamen plant in your kitchen to ward the family and to encourage Hecate's blessings. Grow deep purple and black pansies in window boxes to encourage the planetary vibrations of Saturn. Let ivy grow up the walls of your home for even more bewitching security.

Don't forget to check out the Daily Spell Worksheet on page 187. Write down some ideas for your own individual and custom-made magics. For example, what other plants, crystals, and stones do you enjoy working with that were not listed in these chapters? How do you imagine you could creatively integrate them?

If you want to expand your magical skills, then start learning how to incorporate all of this daily magical information in a whole new way. This includes the knowledge you already have and the new day-by-day correspondences that were presented in this book. Put your own unique spin on things. Decide what your enchanting specialties are. Try creating even more tarot spells, just for you. Craft your own quick candle spells and write your own colorful charms and daily incantations.

Every day is a magical day. Just how bewitching of a day it turns out to be is completely up to you. Shake things up! Work a few quick and personalized spells. Make copies of the spell worksheet and get busy! Advance your skills by teaching yourself new daily enchantments and adding more advanced, custom-made magics and techniques to your repertoire.

Now, take these daily correspondences and fresh ideas from this little book and fly with them. Be creative and stand out as the talented magical individual you are. Just imagine what fantastic things you can achieve every single day of the bewitching week!

Brightest blessings and best wishes on your spellwork!

Each day comes bearing its own gifts.

Untie the ribbons.

Ruth Ann Schabacker

✋

Daily Spell Worksheet

DAY: _____

GOAL: _____

DEITY INVOKED: _____

HERBS USED AND THEIR MAGICAL APPLICATION: _____

_____

CANDLE COLOR: _____

CRYSTALS OR STONES: _____

COORDINATING TAROT CARDS: _____

CHARM: _____

_____

SETUP (EQUIPMENT, SUCH AS CANDLEHOLDERS, A VASE, A

CAULDRON, ETC.): _____

_____

_____

RESULTS: _____

_____

_____

_____

_____

Days of the Week in Old English and Gaelic

This list is simply for fun; I thought it would amuse you!

DAYS OF THE WEEK IN GAELIC (AND PRONUNCIATION)

Sunday	Domhnach *(dow-neg)*
Monday	Luan *(loo-in)*
Tuesday	Mairt *(martch)*
Wednesday	Ceadaoin *(kay-deen)*
Thursday	Deardaoin *(jeyr-deen)*
Friday	Aoine *(hayn-ya)*
Saturday	Sathairn *(sa-harn)*

OLD ENGLISH NAMES FOR THE DAYS OF THE WEEK

AND THEIR MEANINGS

Sunday	Sunnandaeg, "day of the sun"
Monday	Monandaeg, "day of the moon"
Tuesday	Tiwesdaeg, "Tiw's day"
Wednesday	Wodnesdaeg, "Woden's day"
Thursday	Thunresdaeg, "thunder's day" or "Thor's day"
Friday	Frigedaeg, "Freya's day"
Saturday	Saeturnesdaeg, "Saturn's day"

Bibliography

Almond, Jocelyn, and Keith Seddon. *Understanding Tarot: A Practical Guide to Tarot Card Reading.* London, UK: Aquarian Press, 1991.

Aswynn, Freya. *Northern Mysteries and Magick.* St. Paul, MN: Llewellyn, 1998.

Biziou, Barbara. *The Joy of Ritual.* New York, NY: Golden Books, 1999.

Bremness, Lesley. *Herbs.* New York, NY: Dorling Publishing, Inc., 1994.

Bowes, Susan. *Notions and Potions: A Safe Practical Guide to Creating Magick and Miracles.* New York, NY: Sterling Publishing Company, 1997.

Budapest, Zsuzsanna. *The Goddess in the Office.* San Francisco, CA: HarperSanFrancisco, 1993.

Conway, D. J. *Moon Magick.* St. Paul, MN: Llewellyn, 1995.

Cunningham, Scott. *Cunningham's Encyclopedia of Magical Herbs.* St. Paul, MN: Llewellyn, 1996.

———. *Cunningham's Encyclopedia of Crystal, Gem & Metal Magic.* St. Paul, MN: Llewellyn, 1992.

———. *Magical Aromatherapy.* St. Paul, MN: Llewellyn, 1993.

Dugan, Ellen. *Elements of Witchcraft: Natural Magick for Teens.* St. Paul, MN: Llewellyn, 2003.

————. *Garden Witchery: Magick from the Ground Up.* St. Paul, MN: Llewellyn, 2003.

————. *Llewellyn's Herbal Almanac 2004.* "The Rose." St. Paul, MN: Llewellyn, 2003.

————. *Llewellyn's Magickal Almanac 2003.* "Lilith." St. Paul, MN: Llewellyn, 2002.

————. *Llewellyn's Magical Almanac 2004.* "Aphrodite." St. Paul, MN: Llewellyn, 2003.

Dunkling, Leslie. *A Dictionary of Days.* New York, NY: Facts on File Publication, 1988.

Ferguson, Diana. *The Magickal Year.* New York, NY: Book of the Month Club (originally UK: Labyrinth Publishing), 1996.

Gundarsson, Kveldulf. *Teutonic Magic.* St. Paul, MN: Llewellyn, 1994.

Hallam, Elizabeth. *Gods and Goddesses: A Treasury of Deities and Tales from World Mythology.* New York, NY: Simon and Schuster, 1996.

Helfman, Elizabeth S. *Celebrating Nature: Rites and Ceremonies Around the World.* New York, NY: Seabury Press, 1969.

Jordan, Michael. *The Encyclopedia of Gods.* London, Great Britain: Kyle Cathie Limited, 1995.

Bibliography

Laufer, Geraldine Adamich. *Tussie-Mussies: The Victorian Art of Expressing Yourself In the Language of Flowers.* New York, NY: Workman Publishing Company, 1993.

Mercante, Anthony S. *The Magic Garden.* New York, NY: Harper and Row Publishers, 1976.

Monaghan, Patricia. *The Book of Goddesses and Heroines.* St. Paul, MN: Llewellyn, 1981.

Myth and Mankind: Sagas of the Norsemen. Amsterdam: Time-Life Books (First English Printing), 1997.

O'Rush, Claire. *The Enchanted Garden.* New York, NY: Gramercy Books, 2000.

Osborn, Kevin, and Dana L. Burgess, Ph.D. *The Complete Idiot's Guide to Classical Mythology.* New York, NY: Alpha Books, 1998.

Patterson, Jacqueline Memory. *Tree Wisdom.* London, UK: Thorsons, 1996.

Perl, Lila. *Blue Monday and Friday the Thirteenth: The Stories Behind the Days of the Week.* New York, NY: Clarion Books, 1986.

RavenWolf, Silver. *Silver's Spells for Prosperity.* St. Paul, MN: Llewellyn, 1999.

Redford, Donald, B., editor. *The Ancient Gods Speak: A Guide to Egyptian Religion.* New York, NY: Oxford University Press, 2002.

Rossbach, Sarah, and Lin Yun. *Living Color: Master Lin Yun's Guide to Feng Shui and the Art of Color.* New York, NY: Kodansha International, 1994.

Skolnick, Solomon M. *The Language of Flowers.* White Plains, NY: Peter Pauper Press, Inc., 1995.

Starhawk. *The Spiral Dance.* 10th Anniversary Edition. San Francisco, CA: HarperSanFrancisco, 1989.

Telesco, Patricia. *Folkways.* St. Paul, MN: Llewellyn, 1995.

Vitale, Alice Thoms. *Leaves: In Myth, Magic and Medicine.* New York, NY: Stewart, Tabori and Chang, 1997.

Walker, Barbara G. *The Woman's Dictionary of Symbols and Sacred Objects.* Edison, NJ: Castle Books, 1988.

Index

Index

Index

Index

LLEWELLYN ORDERING INFORMATION

 Order Online:
Visit our website at www.llewellyn.com, select your books, and order them on our secure server.

 Order by Phone:
- Call toll-free within the U.S. at 1-877-NEW-WRLD (1-877-639-9753). Call toll-free within Canada at 1-866-NEW-WRLD (1-866-639-9753)
- We accept VISA, MasterCard, and American Express

 Order by Mail:
Send the full price of your order (MN residents add 7% sales tax) in U.S. funds, plus postage & handling to:
Llewellyn Worldwide
P.O. Box 64383, Dept. 0-7387-0589-6
St. Paul, MN 55164-0383, U.S.A.

Postage & Handling:

Standard (U.S., Mexico, & Canada). If your order is:
Up to $25.00, add $3.50
$25.01 - $48.99, add $4.00
$49.00 and over, FREE STANDARD SHIPPING
(Continental U.S. orders ship UPS. AK, HI, PR, & P.O. Boxes ship USPS 1st class. Mex. & Can. ship PMB.)

International Orders:
Surface Mail: For orders of $20.00 or less, add $5 plus $1 per item ordered. For orders of $20.01 and over, add $6 plus $1 per item ordered.

Air Mail:
Books: Postage & Handling is equal to the total retail price of all books in the order.
Non-book items: Add $5 for each item.

Orders are processed within 2 business days.
Please allow for normal shipping time. Postage and handling rates subject to change.

GARDEN WITCHERY

Magick from the Ground Up

(Includes a Gardening Journal)

Ellen Dugan

How does your magickal garden grow? *Garden Witchery* is more than belladonna and wolfs-bane. It's about making your own enchanted backyard with the trees, flowers, and plants found growing around you. It's about creating your own flower fascinations and spells, and it's full of common-sense information about cold hardiness zones, soil requirements, and a realistic listing of accessible magickal plants.

There may be other books on magickal gardening, but none have practical gardening advice, magickal correspondences, flower folklore, moon gardening, faerie magick, advanced witchcraft, and humorous personal anecdotes all rolled into one volume.

0-7387-0318-4, 272 pp., 7½ x 7½, $16.95

ELEMENTS OF WITCHCRAFT
Natural Magick for Teens
Ellen Dugan

A teen primer on the theory, techniques, and tools of natural magick.

Being a witch is not just about casting spells. It's also about magick—the magick of nature and of life. This book, by a veteran witch and mother of three teenagers, shows teens how natural magick is both quietly beautiful and unstoppably powerful, and how they can harness that energy to better their own lives.

The young seeker will be introduced to the theory of witchcraft, the God and the Goddess, and ethical considerations. There are elemental meditations, correspondence charts, information on nature spirits, magickal herbalism, spells, and charms. Teens will also learn how to create their own magickal tools and altars with natural supplies, cast a circle, avoid magickal mistakes, and live a magickal life.

0-7387-0393-1, 336 pp., 6 x 9, illus.   **$14.95**

THE CIRCLE WITHIN
Dianne Sylvan

Anyone can put on a robe and dance the night away at a Sabbat, but it takes courage and discipline to be a Wiccan twenty-four hours a day, seven days a week, for the rest of your life. Every act can be a ritual, and every moment is another chance to honor the Divine. This book shows you how to do just that.

The Circle Within guides the practicing witch toward integrating Wiccan values into his or her real life. The first part of the book addresses the philosophy, practice, and foundations of a spiritual life. The second part is a mini-devotional filled with prayers and rituals that you can use as a springboard to creating your own.

0-7387-0348-6, 264 pp., 5³⁄₁₆ x 8   **$12.95**

THE ELEMENTS OF RITUAL
Air, Fire, Water & Earth in the Wiccan Circle
Deborah Lipp

Wicca 202: Advanced training by an experienced High Priestess.

Many books may tell you how to cast a Wiccan circle, but none really bother to explain why. When you finish reading *The Elements of Ritual*, you'll know what each step of the circle-casting ceremony means, why it's there, and what it accomplishes. You'll learn several alternative approaches to each step, and you'll be empowered to write your own effective ceremonies using sound magical, theological, and pragmatic principles.

0-7387-0301-X, 312 pp., 7½ x 9⅛, illus.   **$16.95**

GREEN WITCHCRAFT
Folk Magic, Fairy Lore & Herb Craft
Aoumiel

Very little has been written about traditional family practices of the Old Religion simply because such information has not been offered for popular consumption. If you have no contacts with these traditions, *Green Witchcraft* will meet your need for a practice based in family and natural Witchcraft traditions.

Green Witchcraft describes the worship of nature and the use of herbs that have been part of human culture from the earliest times. It relates to the Lord and Lady of Greenwood, the Primal Father and Mother, and to the Earth Spirits called Faeries.

Green Witchcraft traces the historic and folk background of this path and teaches its practical techniques. Learn the basics of Witchcraft from a third-generation, traditional family Green Witch who openly shares from her own experiences. Through a how-to format you'll learn rites of passage, activities for Sabbats and Esbats, Fairy lore, self-dedication, self-initiation, spellwork, herbcraft, and divination.

This practical handbook is an invitation to explore, identify and adapt the Green elements of Witchcraft that work for you, today.

1–56718–690–4, 288 pp., 6 x 9, illus.   **$14.95**

THE WAY OF FOUR

Create Elemental Balance in Your Life

Deborah Lipp

Which element are you?

Earth, Air, Fire, and Water—not only are these elements the building blocks of the universe, but also potent keys to heightened self-understanding. *The Way of Four* helps you determine which of the four elements are prominent and which are lacking in your world using a variety of custom-made quizzes. It includes a multitude of methods to incorporate and balance the elements in your environment, wardrobe, and even your perfume. This is a fun and valuable sourcebook for anyone seeking balance and beauty in a hectic world.

0–7387–0541–1, 336 pp., 7½ x 9⅛, illus.   **$17.95**

THE OUTER TEMPLE OF WITCHCRAFT

Circles, Spells, and Rituals

Christopher Penczak

As you enter the heart of witchcraft, you find at its core the power of sacred space. In Christopher Penczak's first book, *The Inner Temple of Witchcraft*, you found the sacred space within yourself. Now *The Outer Temple of Witchcraft* helps you manifest the sacred in the outer world through ritual and spellwork. The book's twelve lessons, with exercises, rituals, and homework, follow the traditional Wiccan one-year-and-a-day training period. It culminates in a self-test and self-initiation ritual to the second degree of witchcraft—the arena of the priestess and priest.

0–7387–0531–4, 448 pp., 7½ x 9⅛, illus.   **$17.95**

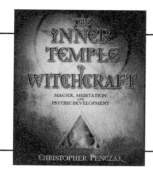

THE INNER TEMPLE OF WITCHCRAFT

Magick, Meditation & Psychic Development

Christopher Penczak

Enter the inner temple and discover the power of your magick! For the serious seeker, *The Inner Temple of Witchcraft* lays the foundation for deep experience with ritual. Instead of diving right into spellwork, this book sets the student on a course of experience with energy and psychic ability—the cornerstones of magick. You will explore witchcraft's ancient history and modern traditions, discovering the path that suits you best. The thirteen lessons take the student through meditation, instant magic, ancient philosophy, modern science, protection, light, energy anatomy, astral travel, spirit guides, and healing, culminating in a self-initiation ritual.

0-7387-0276-5, 352 pp., 7½ x 9⅛   **$17.95**

To Write to the Author

If you wish to contact the author or would like more information about this book, please write to the author in care of Llewellyn Worldwide and we will forward your request. Both the author and publisher appreciate hearing from you and learning of your enjoyment of this book and how it has helped you. Llewellyn Worldwide cannot guarantee that every letter written to the author can be answered, but all will be forwarded. Please write to:

Ellen Dugan
⁒ Llewellyn Worldwide
P.O. Box 64383, Dept. 0-7387-0589-6
St. Paul, MN 55164-0383, U.S.A.

Please enclose a self-addressed stamped envelope for reply,
or $1.00 to cover costs. If outside U.S.A., enclose
international postal reply coupon.

Many of Llewellyn's authors have websites with additional information and resources. For more information, please visit our website:

HTTP://WWW.LLEWELLYN.COM